GLIMMER TRAIN STORIES

EDITORS
Susan Burmeister
Linda Davies

ASSISTANT EDITOR
Scott Allie

EDITORIAL ASSISTANT
Florence McMullen

COMPUTER WIZARD
Michael Brown

DESIGN LAYOUT
Red Rabbit Design

COVER ILLUSTRATION
Jane Zwinger

STORY ILLUSTRATIONS
Jon Leon

LAST PAGE ILLUSTRATION
Bernard Mulligan, Rep. of Ireland

COPY EDITING
Mark Morris

TYPOGRAPHY
Paul O. Giesey/Adcrafters

PUBLISHED QUARTERLY
in February, May, August, and November by
Glimmer Train Press, Inc.
812 SW Washington Street, Suite 1205
Portland, Oregon 97205-3216 U.S.A.
Telephone: 503/221-0836
Facsimile: 503/221-0837

Glimmer Train (ISSN #1055-7520) is published quarterly, $29 per year in the U.S., by Glimmer Train Press, Inc., Suite 1205, 812 SW Washington, Portland, OR 97205. Second class postage paid at Portland, OR. POSTMASTER: Send address changes to Glimmer Train, Suite 1205, 812 SW Washington, Portland, OR 97205.

ISSN # 1055-7520, ISBN # 1-880966-03-4, CPDA BIPAD # 79021

Printed on recycled, acid-free paper. ✺

Subscription rates: One year, $29 within the U.S.
Air mail to Canada, $39.
Air mail outside North America, $49.
Payable by Visa/MC or check for U.S. dollars drawn on a U.S. bank.

Attention short-story writers: *We pay $300 for first publication and one-time anthology rights. We pay an additional $300 if your story is chosen for publication in our anthology. Please include a self-addressed, sufficiently stamped envelope with your submission.* **Manuscripts accepted in January, April, July, and October.** *Send a SASE for guidelines.*

Dedication

We dedicate this issue
to all of you who have embraced Glimmer Train
by sending in your work and by subscribing,

to Scott Allie, Michael Brown, and Florence McMullen,
with admiration and fondness,

and
to the human race
in this important final decade
of the millennium.

Our first year has ended.
Here's to Year Two.

Susan Burmeister   Linda Davies

CONTENTS

CONTENTS

Janice Rosenberg

This picture of me at age eight was taken on an unidentified, but typical, Chicago street. The dog's name is Moishe Pupik, which means something like Moses's Navel. He was named after a hot-dog stand. I took him everywhere with me in lieu of a real dog and made up stories about "Dogland," the country that he came from. Back then I had a nice smile and messy bangs, and I still do.

Free-lance writer Janice Rosenberg has lived in Chicago all her life. She is married and has two sons who are both in college "and one German shepherd dog who is not." Rosenberg's stories have appeared in *Seventeen, Aurora, Other Voices, My Weekly, Amelia, Emrys Journal, Arts Alive,* and the *Albany Review.* Her nonfiction articles appear in publications ranging from *Ladies' Home Journal* to *American Medical News.* She is one of six authors of *Reinventing Home* (Plume, March 1991), a book of essays written in "workshop-style"; a sequel, *Reinventing Love,* is to be published in February 1993.

Janice Rosenberg

JANICE ROSENBERG
Chance of a Lifetime

*V*era Goldman sits at the kitchen table pouring white liquid through a funnel into a tube connected to a surgically created opening in her stomach. She wears a flowered night-gown, hiked up, with a towel draped across her exposed thighs. Her husband Harry is in the living room sorting through a stack of mail. She can hear him tearing envelopes and unfolding letters.

When she turns on the water in the sink he comes into the kitchen, his house shoes shuffling over the linoleum. "You ready to watch?" he asks.

In the bedroom Harry sits in an armchair on her side of the connected twin beds. She eases under the covers, propping two pillows behind her. An airline commercial fills the TV screen with sky, then a camera pans an excited audience behind script lettering that reads: *The Million Dollar Chance of a Lifetime.* Harry started watching this show when she was in the hospital for the surgery. Each evening two couples compete in a complicated electronic version of hang man.

Harry points to the couple on the right. "This is their second night," he says, as if she didn't know.

The show's host reintroduces Christine and Jeffrey Renaldi. They are young, from Queens. Any children? "Not yet," Christine says, smiling. She does something secretarial and he's a postal worker. Vera rooted for them the night before. Always one of the couples appeals to her more than the other. The Renaldis—enthusiastic, quick-witted—stood out right away.

When the game begins, Vera concentrates on the board, trying out different letters, aware of certain patterns in the titles and phrases. "The second word could be *in* or *on*," she says.

Harry grunts. He rarely contributes, but then he has never been good at guessing games—charades or twenty questions—the way she is. What he likes about this show is seeing people win money.

During a commercial he asks, "Did Bessie Weiner call? Sam said they'd stop by on the weekend."

"She called. But she's not coming."

"She's not? Go on. What are you talking about? Sam said they'd be in town and they'd stop by."

"I talked to her. It makes her too nervous."

"What does? Sam said—"

"Sh. It's back."

The show returns. The Renaldis win. Now comes the most exciting part. The host ushers the couple into a glass booth. Whispering together behind their hands, they choose their category: "Cars." They have just sixty seconds to puzzle out six words.

At first Vera could not believe it when Harry told her some people managed to accomplish this. But by now she has seen it happen more than once. Tonight she holds her breath as the Renaldis struggle to fill in "Oldsmobile" and "Jaguar." They leave the booth triumphant, their young faces rosy with effort. They can quit and take their money or come back tomorrow night. Without hesitating they say in unison that they'll be back.

"They're good," Harry says. "They both work with words, maybe that's why. So what's with Bessie?"

"Nothing. She just can't stand to be with sick people, that's all. It makes her nervous."

"Did she tell you that or are you guessing?"

"She told me, Harry. It makes her nervous. So they're not coming. What difference does it make?"

"Son of a bitch," he mumbles, his favorite oath. "Sam tells me and then he lets her decide..."

Vera watches him thumb through the television listings. She can tell he's too hurt by Sam's defection to think of how she must feel about Bessie.

The next night Christine Renaldi wears her long dark hair pinned up. Jeffrey smiles at the back of her neck when it's her turn to do the puzzle. She pats his arm as they exchange places. Vera imagines them getting ready for the show in their small, hot apartment. Christine straightens Jeffrey's tie. He admires her new dress, white splashed with vivid pastel flowers. They are both too excited to eat dinner. We'll have something afterward, he tells her. They hold hands on the subway.

Imagining, Vera misses the second round, in which the Renaldis lose to their challengers, a couple named Edgar and Jane something. The third round begins. Vera digs her nails into her palms, concentrating. The challengers falter and the Renaldis win.

Once again in the glass booth they whisper behind their hands. This time they choose "Candy." They pass after a few seconds' effort on the first word.

"It's licorice," Vera says as the next clues appear.

"Go on," Harry says. "You couldn't tell so fast."

"Licorice," she repeats. "You'll see."

The Renaldis complete the rest of the words in record time—peppermint, taffy, lollypop, caramel—then return to the first. In the last second, Jeffrey, grinning, calmly says, "Licorice."

"Yes, we'll come back," the Renaldis tell the host. "Of course we'll come back."

Harry switches to a situation comedy. With her eyes closed Vera imagines the Renaldis walking up Sixth Avenue outside the television studio. They are talking of how they will spend the million dollars. Of course they must win twice more for the grand prize, but that doesn't stop them from sharing their dreams.

Christine wants to quit her job and have a baby. Jeffrey says he will continue delivering mail, but at the same time he will use some of the money to start the business he has always wanted. What business is that, Vera wonders. What would a postal carrier choose to do? Her own son is an accountant, her daughter a psychologist. All the young people she knows go to graduate school. In any case, the Renaldis will want a house.

Not that people can't raise children in apartments. Vera raised both of hers on the tenth floor overlooking Broadway. How sweet they both were as infants, as energetic toddlers running up and down the apartment's long hallway, even as teenagers. She spent their early years chatting with the neighborhood women in Riverside Park. It would be nice to go there now, to walk along the paths in the summer dusk. If it weren't for Harry she would shut off the air-conditioning and open the bedroom windows. She would let in the New York soot, the traffic noises, the breeze that lifts Christine's hair as she and Jeffrey walk along arm in arm, their steps synchronized. They stop of one accord in front of a department store window. The striped couch,

Jeffrey says, and Christine nods, wide-eyed: Perfect.

Vera stares at Harry, engrossed now in television crime fighting. I'd like the windows open, she radios, putting the full force of her will behind the thought. Nothing happens until the station break. Then he looks up and says, "I'll do the marketing tomorrow."

She dozes and wakes to the ten o'clock news. During the sports report she goes into the bathroom. When she comes out Harry is in the living room reading. He has always liked staying up late. She is used to going to bed without him. She calls good night. They do not kiss. They have not kissed in years. She tries to remember kissing him, but cannot. He has a heavy beard. When they were courting he shaved a second time before he came to see her after work.

They met at a party. Harry and a friend of his were going to Europe for two months, using every penny they had. The daring of it impressed her. He wasn't afraid to leave his job. There would be others, he said. He was almost thirty and he wanted to travel before settling down.

After the party he walked her home. At her building he asked if he could write to her. He scribbled her address on the inside of a nearly empty matchbook. Upstairs, she looked out of the window and watched him light a cigarette. As he walked up the street, she imagined him tossing the matchbook into the trash. Three weeks later an airmail letter from London surprised her. She had forgotten his name.

Having been awake on and off all night, Vera sleeps late. The phone wakes her at nine-thirty.

"Good morning, sleepyhead," her sister Florence says. "How is my baby sister feeling today?"

"Give me a minute to think, Flo," Vera says.

She puts her hand over the receiver and coughs. Her mouth is dry. The pain in her stomach has become a constant, a stitch that keeps her bent in the middle. Sometimes for an hour she sleeps and forgets it, like the twilight sleep they gave her when she had the children. She remembers sleeping, oblivious, then waking to the next contraction with no time to prepare herself.

"Vera darling," Flo says. "Tell me. Did you talk to the doctor like I told you?"

"I talked to him. He said to add more water to the formula. It's better."

"No cramps?"

"No cramps," she lies. Flo knows that she's dying even though she pretends otherwise.

"What about the children?" Flo asks. "They called?"

"What do you think? Of course they called," Vera says. "Rochelle is coming this weekend. Lawrence was just here, remember?"

"Of course I remember. Isn't he my favorite nephew?"

"He's your favorite. He's also your only," Vera says as always. "Will I see you today?"

"Around noon. I'm making you some soup. And don't argue. The doctor said you should try to eat. You'll see how good it's going to taste."

"I'll see," Vera says. She has given up trying to convince Flo not to cook for her. It makes Flo feel good and that counts for something. "You'll help me wash my hair."

"I'll help. Good-bye Vera darling. See you later."

Vera goes into the kitchen and sits down to feed herself. Harry is out somewhere, doing the marketing perhaps. He and Flo never got along. They were too much alike: independent, decisive, what they call nowadays goal-oriented. Flo went to nursing school over their parents' objections. Then she quit to marry Morris, positive that he was what she wanted. Morris was a lawyer, a night school graduate, seven years older than Flo, already bald at twenty-five. Again their parents objected, but it turned out they were wrong. Everybody said Flo and Morris had a wonderful marriage. Vera, seeing it up close, knew they did.

Why deny it? She envies her sister, for her marriage, her strength, her vivacious personality. By the time Vera met Harry, the family was certain that she would be an old maid. Twenty-three and still at home, working for a dentist. Her parents liked Harry. A go-getter, her father called him. You could do worse, her mother said.

Now he comes in carrying a bag of groceries. "I got the applesauce." He sets the jar on the table.

She checks the label: Extra smooth. "Thank you. No, don't put it in the refrigerator. Leave it on the counter."

After he empties his bag he goes into the living room with the newspaper. "You just get up?" he asks.

"Half an hour ago," she answers. "Flo is coming at noon."

Although she's unable to see him, she can picture his mouth pulling into a straight line of automatic disapproval. He mumbles something that she can't make out.

"I have books to return at the library," he says. Then, "Fred Cohen sends regards. They're going up to the mountains for a week. It's been so hot here."

"Is it better today?"

"No. Hot. Not a breeze."

And only June, Vera thinks. She and Harry used to go to the Berkshires every summer, for music at Tanglewood and dancing at Jacob's Pillow. Harry's choices. For the first time that day she remembers the Renaldis. If they take a summer vacation it will be to visit Christine's sister in Rochester. Vera has no idea why that comes into her head. Nevertheless it makes her smile.

Later, Flo helps Vera take a shower. She combs Vera's hair. "You should go down to the beauty shop. It'll do you good."

"It's a long walk," Vera says.

"A long walk." Flo stands with her fists on her hips. "A long walk. So? You'll take a taxi. I'll take you. What's the number?"

Vera opens her address book and Flo makes an appointment for the following Tuesday. By then, Vera thinks, the Renaldis may have won their million dollars. She doesn't tell Flo about them. Her sister would think that she was crazy, talking about people from a game show.

While Flo reports the latest on her son's divorce, Vera finds herself picturing the Renaldis in bed together. The erotic nature of this image does not disturb her as it once would have. Dying has made all kinds of previously forbidden thoughts possible and surprisingly pleasurable. No longer hearing Flo, she settles deeper into her fantasy.

The Renaldis finish making love and lie under a sheet in the twilight of their bedroom, smiling into each other's eyes. Christine's hair hangs in waves over her bare shoulders. Jeffrey touches her cheek. You are beautiful, he tells her. She looks away shyly, then cuddles close against him despite the heat. Soon they will dress and go out for a stroll, an ice cream cone...

"Vera," Flo says sharply. "You're not listening. Here, take a taste of this soup."

"What is it?"

Flo glares at her with her familiar mock angry frown. "Always daydreaming. I told you. Fish chowder. Look, I made it nice and smooth." She spoons some up and tries to feed Vera.

"I can do it myself," Vera tells her.

"Good. Then do it. I have to go home." She takes off her apron and bends to kiss Vera's cheek. "Make Harry help you, darling. Tell him I said so."

"A million dollars used to mean you were a millionaire," Harry says that evening as they wait through a long string of commercials for the show to begin. "Now, even if you can invest it at five and three-quarters, it's not enough to live on in style. You need at least five million for that."

"We wouldn't have sneezed at it."

"No. Are you kidding? A million dollars fifty years ago..." He rolls his eyes at the ceiling. "That would've put you right up there with Rockefeller."

Tonight Christine wears a corsage of pink roses pinned to her dress. She says that Jeffrey bought it for good luck. They squeeze hands then take their separate places. For a time the score goes back and forth, but in the end the Renaldis win.

This time in the booth they select "Vegetables." As the clock ticks, Jeffrey shouts "eggplant" correctly when only the *p* and *t* are filled in. Christine supplies "artichoke" as soon as the *ch* shows up. The final word stumps them.

"Rutabaga," Vera says.

"Is that right?" Harry spells aloud. "Rutabaga. No kidding."

The young couple stands tense and silent, lips moving. Vera is mad at the game show people. Who eats rutabagas anymore? Then suddenly Christine says it as if nothing could be more obvious. Amidst cheers and whistles they agree to come back for the jackpot.

"Rutabagas," Harry says as the theme music swells. "The Korean sells them. I don't think I ever ate one."

"It's a kind of turnip," Vera says. "Mama put them in soup sometimes."

He checks his watch ostentatiously. "The men's club is having a speaker tonight. I read about it in the synagogue bulletin. It sounded interesting, but I don't know. I wouldn't get home until late..."

"Go," she tells him. Can he think she needs his meager company? "I'll manage."

With no further demurrals he retrieves his sport coat and hat from the bedroom closet. He never goes out without them, even if he's only going for the newspaper. He was always a sharp dresser, something she noticed right away. On their first date he wore a light summer suit, a straw hat, and those spectator shoes he liked so much. They went to the movies. He told her about

Hitler. Everyone said there would be a war before long. He was glad he'd taken the time to visit the shtetl in Poland where his cousins lived. That kind of life will be over soon, he said prophetically, except he meant they would all be in America, not dead.

Within a week of his return, Harry had a job as assistant pharmacist in a drugstore in Washington Heights. He was ambitious, talked about owning his own store. Vera admired that. He was smart, too. When they walked in Central Park he explained history to her. She thought that after they were married he would learn to take her arm at corners, to hold her coat and compliment her hats. When they could be alone together in their own apartment he would romance her. She counted on him, as a man, to know what they should do in bed, and of course he did. Timid, embarrassed, ignorant of female sexuality—what her daughter the therapist would call re-pressed—she waited patiently those first few years to feel an overwhelming passion.

At three a.m. Vera wakens to Harry's snoring. The pain won't let her lie still. She swallows a pill with a tiny bit of tepid water. In the living room she stands at the window looking down twenty stories onto Second Avenue. Ten years ago they moved here from the West Side. Day and night, cars and taxis never stop. It's as if they ride a conveyor belt from Washington Heights down to the Bowery and then pass under the island and pop up again. She watches the traffic lights change sequentially until she is hypnotized.

Taking a blanket from the hall closet, she lies on the couch, knees drawn up against the pain. What does it matter, being up all night if she has nothing to do the next day? That is the oddest part about being sick. Before, she volunteered twice a week at the Jewish welfare resale shop. Harry made fun of her for taking the work seriously. "What's the matter," he asked when she refused to skip a day. "You afraid they'll fire you?" He never approved of wives working. But after they were married she continued at the dentist's office because they needed the money. She worked for three years, until their first baby was well on the way.

Closing her eyes Vera sees the dentist, Dr. Lyons, sitting on the black leatherette couch in his waiting room. He offers his package of Sen Sen. She holds out her hand and he pours in several of the tiny chips. Then his fingers touch hers and their eyes meet. A shiver passes over her, then and now. Was that before or after Harry? Dr. Lyons was married, of course. And he never made a real pass at her, otherwise she could not have worked there. He gave her a large bonus as a wedding gift. A nice man, generous, he has been dead for years.

She shifts on the couch, looking for a comfortable position even though she knows there is none. It's amazing how her thoughts drift. Just when she thinks she has nothing left to think about, whole new areas open up. Lately she has thought often of her parents, her childhood. When they were small girls in Russia, she and Flo shared a bed. In her memories of that time it is always winter and they lie huddled together against the cold. She falls asleep soothed by that ancient comfort.

The next night Vera finishes with her feeding half an hour before the show. To pass the time she puts on a fresh nightgown and brushes her hair. Her face is so thin, so wrinkled, her body emaciated. An ugly word, she thinks, *emaciated*. She was always a small person, but now she resembles a very old fleshless child. Both breasts had to be removed two years earlier. The scars healed in bumpy curves.

If this happened to Christine, she wonders, would Jeffrey still love her? But the thing is, Harry never loved her in the first place. He married her only because she turned up just when he wanted to settle down. And vice versa, she admits to herself. She tries to recall the happiness she must have felt when he asked her to marry him. All that she can remember is a feeling of intense relief.

They settle into their usual places in the bedroom. When the show starts, hands under the covers, Vera crosses her fingers. She tries to give the Renaldis' opponents what her grandmother called the evil eye. Whether or not it works, the challengers seem awed, as if Christine and Jeffrey possess some kind of magic. In fact, they win by a wide margin.

"This is it," Harry says as they step into the glass booth for the last time. The subjects are announced. "I think they made them harder tonight," he says. "The sponsors can't be in such a big hurry to give away a million dollars."

"That wouldn't be fair," Vera says as the Renaldis whisper together.

"What's fair? We're talking about business here, not just a game."

The Renaldis quickly choose "National Parks." Vera wipes her sweaty palms on the sheet. Foolish, she thinks. These people are strangers. But they do not feel like strangers. They smile at the camera, at each other, at her. Right now Vera would *pay* a million dollars—if she had it—to change places with Christine.

Tears fill her eyes, but she has no time to think. The words begin, coming faster than ever.

"Yellowstone," Vera says just before Christine gets it. "Skip to the next one," she urges when they stall momentarily. "Yosemite," she says simultaneously with Jeffrey.

Her heart beats faster as the seconds tick away. She is unaware of her pain, of Harry's presence in the bedroom. Only the Renaldis matter. They work efficiently, deciphering words like a pair of code breakers trying to save their country. Until the last word appears. Just five spaces long, it stumps them: _R _CE. So simple this time that even Harry gets it, but then he's always been interested in geography.

"Bryce." He flaps a hand at the screen in disgust. "They've probably never been west of the Hudson, that's all."

And that is how it ends. In the television studio the audience sighs. Inside the booth, Christine rests her head on Jeffrey's shoulder. He curves his arm around her and they hold each other as if they have forgotten all the people watching.

The show's host opens the door. "Good try," he says. "Not very many people get this far. Consolation prizes," he says, naming this and that. Vera is not listening. She is thinking that after the show the Renaldis will have dinner with their families in Little Italy. They will drink wine and tell each other that it doesn't matter, that nothing matters as long as they have each other.

The theme music plays as cheerfully as ever. The three stand waving good-bye behind bright script: *Million Dollar Chance of a Lifetime*.

"Oh, well," Harry says. "That was plenty exciting. They'll get over it. After all, they have their health and they have each other."

A wistful quality in his voice makes her turn to him. For a long moment—longer than it took the Renaldis to know that they would never guess that last word—she looks into his eyes. She imagines telling him about her peculiar affection for the young couple, about her vicarious pleasure in their togetherness, about everything. I'm frightened, Harry, she could say. I need to know you'll miss me when I'm gone. Hold me, she could say, and—most fantastic of all—make love to me.

Harry waits, for once not rushing to adjust the television. Emotions file across his face: helplessness despair disgust fear loneliness frustration. She reads them easily, could win a prize if one were being offered. Instead, she closes her eyes. The pages of the TV listings rustle. Then the channel changer clicks and the room fills with the mocking reverberations of recorded laughter.

Cathie Beck

TREK might have begged me to endorse their product—offering me a flashy aluminum bike, high-tech helmet, the works. But I could not have been talked into wearing that black Spandexy stuff—you know—fluorescent pink stripes squeezing my thighs, a sports bra the size of your thumb. No, it was strictly Bitchin' Baby Biking Britches for me.

Cathie Beck has held the following jobs: columnist, waitress, critic, bartender, and baton-twirling teacher. She is a free-lance writer currently working on a novel and collection of short stories.

Beck said that when she is not waiting in lines, she teaches literature in St. Petersburg, Russia, and writes long letters home.

CATHIE BECK
Español

*H*e was our only source of income. We walked at least a block behind him. Always. That was our safety range. Most afternoons he stood on Eastern Avenue behind Our Lady of Blessed Redemption Grade School, though Mary Theresa said she saw him on Michigan Street near the kickball diamond sometimes. Mary Theresa was my best friend and the third oldest of twelve children. We were both nine years old that fall.

I did it for the money. I was also the third oldest but we only had six kids. We lived on my dad's seventy-nine-dollar-a-week paycheck, when he brought it home.

Mary Theresa probably did it for similar reasons, though she may have done it for sport. She liked to say smart-aleck things and was the first one of us to cuss out loud. She called Sister Patricia Amadeus a hairy-legged old bitch to her face the first week of school that year and instantly won my respect.

We were always startled to round the Rural Street and Eastern Avenue corner, though he lurked there nearly every afternoon. It made us giddy when we spotted him. He waited for us, patient, and when we finally stopped skipping and pushing and yakking about whether Sister Patricia Amadeus shaved her face or not, he would face us, sullen, standing straight, but never stepping toward us.

His hair, black and slicked back, lay like shiny plastic against his brown skin. I cannot remember his hands or his legs or his feet.

Because he was all coat.

His coat wrapped him from neck to mid-shin like a shroud. It hung to his ankles. It was a tan coat with lots of buttons down the front and a big, wide belt at his waist, though neither was ever fastened. He kept his coat closed by jamming his fists deep in the pockets and crossing his arms in front of him.

I would always pinch Mary Theresa's arm hard when I first spotted him, and then Mary Theresa would shriek and shove me hard on the shoulder. The racket attracted his attention. It was our trio's signal, our method of communicating, and he would shift his weight expectantly.

"You do it!" Mary Theresa said. She was my boss that fall.

"I can't!" I screamed. "He'll get me!" I covered my mouth as the words were meant only for Mary Theresa, though any fool on the block could hear me.

Then I made sure he was looking at me.

"Español?" I said, real quiet. I always said it real low the first time 'cause I was scared. It was a kind of practice, a warm-up.

"He didn't hear you," Mary Theresa said. She had moved back ten paces.

"Shut up, Mary Terry." I always called her Mary Terry when I was mad. "ESS-PANN-YOLE?" I repeated, taunting and hesitant.

He stepped one step toward us. I screamed and jumped back to Mary.

"You've got to get closer," she said and grabbed my wrist and yanked me forward. Then she took over. She stuck her arms out from her sides like a spindly bird and spread her feet a foot or so apart to balance herself. She bent over a little at the waist and poked out her skinny nine-year-old butt.

"ESS-PANN-YOLE?" she called, loud and sing-songy, making the word a sentence of its own. The man did not move.

"ESS-PANN-YOOLLL?" she repeated, and this time she shook her butt back and forth to the beat of the syllables and made circles with her arms and swung her hips wider.

I stood next to her. "Ess-pann-YOLLL," I called. And there we stood, the two of us shoulder to shoulder, our arms spread wide, our mouths open and yelling like hungry baby birds, our butts dancing back and forth. Sometimes when we really got going, we would turn circles on the sidewalk and chant in unison, "Es-pan-yole, we love you! Es-pan-yole, we love you!" We threw him kisses for a finale.

He always waited till the end, till we were done. Then he took one step forward; at the same time, we jumped about three steps back, keeping that full city block between him and us, and he would flip open his coat—wide. Sometimes he flapped it a couple times.

It was the first and last penis I ever saw when I was nine years old. It was the only penis I ever saw from a block away. Mary Theresa had nine brothers, so she had seen lots of them, but she shrieked as loud as me and we both held each other's arms, giggling and hysterical and titillated and ashamed.

That's when Español gave up his quarters. A fistful of them, pulled from the depths of his deep pockets and hurled across the sidewalk. We waited till he left, then raced to the corner and grabbed them, checking the curb for strays.

He kept us in Cokes and Hostess Ding Dongs up till Christmas that year, and we were financially devastated in January when we came back to school and he was gone, though we both had hopes that maybe he had just switched corners on us. It worked out okay in the end, though. Patrick, Mary Theresa's brother, taught us to shoplift in the spring.

Terry Wolverton

*My grandmother used to read to me when I was a little
girl—not just children's stories, but passages from
Shakespeare and poems she'd memorized when she was a
school-teacher. It is from her that I learned the love of
language that inspired me to become a writer.*

Terry Wolverton is a writer of fiction, poetry, drama, and art criticism, which
has been published in periodicals internationally, including the *Jacaranda
Review*, *Fuse*, and *Heresies*. Her work has been anthologized six times. She
recently co-edited *Harbinger: poetry and fiction by Los Angeles writers* (Beyond
Baroque and the Los Angeles Festival) and *Indivisible: short fiction by West Coast
gay and lesbian writers* (New American Library), and has edited *Blood Whispers:
L.A. Writers on AIDS*. She is currently at work on her first novel, *The Labrys
Reunion*.

Since 1976, Wolverton has lived in Los Angeles, where she has been active in
the feminist, gay and lesbian, and art communities. In addition to writing,
Terry has toured North America as a performance artist, and has produced
audio and video art, as well as installations. She has received six California Arts
Council Artist-in-Residence grants in literature, and is the former executive
director of the Woman's Building, a public center for women's culture in Los
Angeles.

TERRY WOLVERTON
A Whisper in the Veins

The apartment is small and ugly modern, and I stand tracking mud and melted snow onto the nondescript linoleum of its tiny kitchen. My mother rises from her rocking chair where she's been reading the paper, padding into the kitchen in her stockinged feet.

I stare at her feet as I remember a story she used to tell me when I was a child. "I always wanted to have fat feet," the story begins. "Mine are skinny and narrow and I thought it would be just wonderful to have fat feet." She never explained where this standard of beauty originated—she takes it for granted that anyone would understand the desire. "So one day I was walking outdoors and I stepped on a bee. I did it on purpose because I knew it would make my foot swell. What I didn't know is that it would be so painful!"

Her arms close around me and I lean down to kiss her cheek. She takes my coat and spreads a newspaper where I can leave my wet shoes. The darkened leather warns me that these Cole-Hahn loafers will never be the same. It wasn't snowing in D.C., where I started from this morning. I tell her I have only the afternoon, a more or less impulsive stopover on my way home from a business trip.

Glimmer Train Stories, Issue 4, Fall 1992
©*1992 Terry Wolverton*

I follow her in my damp socks into the living room. I recognize a few of the pieces of furniture that I grew up with—an old desk, a large oak bureau, my father's stuffed green chair—but they seem unfamiliar in this square room. Against one wall a television is flickering, though the sound is turned down. It's not the same one that I last saw in my parents' house. Most of the furniture is new, bought from Sears or Montgomery Ward on time payments.

I sit in my father's chair. She is anxious and shy with me, bustling around making coffee, tidying up the scattered pieces of the paper, wanting to get me a sweater, though the room isn't cold. She asks if I need to go to the bathroom. I don't. I pick up the front page of the paper and retreat into reading it, sinking into news of a plane crash, a treaty negotiated, the predictions of a dire year for agriculture.

My mother brings me a cup of pale brown coffee. She's always made her coffee weak. "Looks like rain, but it smells like coffee," my father used to joke. She interrupts my reading to ask if I'd like some toast or a cinnamon roll. Monosyllabic, I indicate my preference for the former and begin studying Ann Landers's advice to a woman whose relatives criticize her housekeeping.

After I've scanned the comics, my mother pulls the card table over in front of my chair. The table is draped with a lacy crocheted table cloth, which covers a cotton cloth printed with red cherries. I remember the cherries from the kitchen table in my childhood. She sets a plate of toast on top and moves my coffee cup beside it. I lay the paper aside, pick up a heavily buttered slice of toast and dunk it in my coffee cup. This is something I do only when I'm with my mother. It is her custom, and in her house I observe it.

Little crumbs bob in the cup and a puddle of melted butter creates a rainbow slick on the surface of the coffee. The soaking bread dissolves easily in my mouth.

"How are you? Have you been healthy?" my mother asks, still

shyly. This is an innocent question, standard in my mother's repertoire.

I nod, noncommittally. I'm caught off guard, and glance at her suspiciously. I've come here to tell her something, but I can't just blurt it out to her, not in this small ugly room with the television flickering.

My mother doesn't wait for an answer. Her attention has wandered to the screen, where characters in a soap opera act out their dramas. When I was a child I used to watch these with my mother when I'd stay home from school. I have friends who are too sick to work anymore and they stay home every day and watch the soaps. When they're not talking about their symptoms or a new doctor or the latest experimental treatment, they talk about the stories on the soaps.

"Erica's going to get what's coming to her now," my mother remarks, referring to the woman on the screen whose evil good looks invite fascination and loathing. I don't know what Erica's got coming to her, but I can tell by looking at her she has karmic debts to pay. I've heard Jerry and Stuart talk about Erica, but since I don't follow the soaps, I've never paid much attention.

"How've you been feeling, Mom?" I change the subject.

She starts a little, shifts her attention back to me, and blinks behind her glasses. My mother's never worn glasses before, I realize, and she's picked out a really stupid pair, ones which are not flattering to her face or coloring. They're also at least ten years out of fashion.

It makes me crazy when my mother's cheap. I know that my father left her a comfortable sum of money, but here she is in a drab apartment, shopping at Sears and buying tacky polyester pantsuits and stupid glasses. I really ought to take her shopping.

I used to do that when I was younger. My father was appalled, but as a fifteen-year-old boy I liked nothing better than to take my mother shopping. We'd drive over to one of the better department stores—I always insisted on that—and spend the afternoon amid the racks of women's Sportswear, Better Dresses, Town and Country. My mother was amazed that I had such a sense of women's clothing; I knew fabrics, lines, designer labels. She always swore I had better taste than she did. My mother was still an attractive woman then, and I loved to make her look gorgeous.

Now she has terrible glasses and a bad perm. This makes me sad. It's been a couple of years since I've seen her—the last time was at my father's funeral.

"Oh, I'm all right, I guess. I have such a hard time sleeping," she complains softly in answer to my question. "And I still have these stomach pains when I eat."

"Didn't the doctor tell you to stop drinking coffee?" She has told me this about her stomach in several of our phone conversations. I've tried to call her more regularly since my father died.

"Well, yes, but I don't drink it very much." She is distracted; she really wants to find out what's going to happen to Erica.

My mother and I were very close, up until I was about nineteen. That's when I told her I was gay. She took it hard, a lot harder than my father. I suppose he had always known. It disgusted him, but it wasn't a surprise. I think my mother blamed herself. Maybe she heard my father's hundreds of admonishments—"You're spoiling him, Mae"—and took them to heart for the first time.

Anyway, we'd said some terrible things to each other then, and I upped and moved to L.A. My parents became a distant memory, a photograph. I'd send presents at Christmas and cards on birthdays, but they had no part in my daily life.

The soap ends and my mother moves across the room and presses the button that turns the TV off. The picture disappears from the screen, collapsing in on itself, and the room is suddenly darker. She shuffles to the other corner of the room and turns on a lamp. I recognize the lamp from my father's den in the old house, but as with the other familiar objects in the room it is unfamiliar here.

"Do you want some more coffee," she asks awkwardly, standing by the window with its cheap lace curtains, "or some more toast? Can I make you a tuna sandwich?" She's happy to see me, but doesn't know exactly what to do with me.

"Let's play some cards," I suggest, and she smiles in relief. She indicates for me to lift my plate and saucer, then she peels the crocheted cloth off the table, revealing more fully the faded splendor of the printed cherries below. She goes to the bureau and slides open a drawer, easily finding the deck in its proper place. She pulls a folding chair to the opposite side of the card table, and sits.

The cards are well worn—I recognize the deck with its illustration of hunting dogs on the back. The game is gin rummy, the continuation of a ritual begun in my early childhood. Whenever I'd be home sick, or on nights when my father didn't get home on time, or on holidays when there was no place to go, even on the night of my father's funeral after the guests had gone home—my mother and I would compete for the Gin Rummy Championship of the World.

She liked to devise an elaborate score sheet, with three games at once. If you won a hand, your score was entered in the first game. When you won another hand, that was added to your earlier total while at the same time got you entered into the second game.

Gin rummy brings out a competitive streak that is seldom seen otherwise in either of our personalities. My mother is a cutthroat card player, and she'll watch with cunning which cards I pick up, which I discard, and plan her strategy accordingly.

I spread my hand open in front of my face and sort through: a pair of dark kings and the jack of spades—I can play that either way, hoping for a third king or the queen of spades. I have the four, five, six of clubs. Nothing else to speak of, but I can build from there.

"You," I announce, waving my cards at her, "have dealt me a supreme hand!" We bluff to torment one another. "You really ought to shuffle better."

"One card," she teases back. "Just give me one card."

I once taught this game to Stuart, during one of the bad periods when he was bedridden. It had been hard for him to concentrate and he was easy to beat. I'd felt guilty about winning, but didn't know how not to.

My mother's brow is furrowed as she tries to decide whether to pick up the jack of spades I just discarded or take her chances from the deck. She chooses a new card and her face lights up.

"I'm going to knock with four points!" she crows triumphantly, spreading her cards on top of the cherries.

I lay down my three kings, my four, five, six of clubs. I have two deuces which I toss to the side to offset her four points. I'm still holding the eight of hearts and the ace of diamonds.

"Nine points," I say glumly, and she gleefully records this on her score sheet.

As she deals again I watch her hands. I've always loved my mother's hands. They are strong still, and heavily veined, spotted now with age, but agile as she flips the cards into a pile in front of me.

As has been our custom now for many years, she asks me nothing about my life. "How's your job?" she'll say, expecting and gratified to hear, "Oh, about the same." She'll ask about my house—I've sent her pictures of the Spanish-style home in the Hollywood Hills where Robert and I used to live together—but not about what it's like to live there alone now, or if in fact I am living there alone.

I win the next hand—all the right cards just come to me, as they always seem to do when I don't care about winning—with an extra twenty-five points for ginning. I don't know how I'm going to say what I've come all this way to tell her.

She wants to know if I've seen any movies and we talk about the latest releases. Some of my favorites are independents that won't make it to this part of the country. Outside the window I can see it starting to snow more heavily, and the afternoon is growing dark.

She tells me that my cousin Lenore, her sister's daughter, has had a baby, a boy. She named it Gregory, which is my name, but also my grandfather's. I tell her something cute that my dog Jackson did recently. She smiles vaguely—she doesn't know a lot about dogs.

When Robert got sick, he had to call his parents in Waco, Texas, and tell them for the first time that he was gay. I remember lying in bed that morning, watching his neck flush and the muscles of his back tense as he listened to first his mother, then his father tell him that his illness was God's punishment. That they would pray for him. They never came to visit during those weeks when Robert was in the hospital, and I couldn't decide who he needed me to be most—his lover or his parent.

I want to tell my mother this story, as she quickly grasps the queen of diamonds and positions it in her hand. She discards the five of spades and I pick it up, although I have no use for it at all.

I'm playing recklessly now, totally without strategy, picking up and discarding with no thought for the consequences. When my mother wins, I'm holding seventy-three points in my hand.

She looks at me over the top of those unflattering frames and complains, "You're not concentrating! It's not fun if you make it so easy for me!" She dutifully records that she's won the first game and is perilously close to taking the second as well.

I deal, shuffling the cards automatically. I'm thinking about my test, just a couple of weeks ago, about the earnest counselor who gave me my results. She was wearing green eye shadow that was a bad color for her skin tone, and made more prominent the deep circles under her eyes.

My mother takes this hand easily and throws down her cards

in disgust. "You're worse than your father!" she snorts.

My father was a terrible card player. He was a cabinetmaker, as his father had been, as so many men had once been in this lumber-rich part of the country. He trusted the grain of wood, the burls and knots, what he could see and shape with his own hands. The abstract patterns of clubs and diamonds and their possibilities were never real to him.

"I'm sorry." I smile, conciliatory. I glance at my watch. "I've got a couple more hours. Can I take you out for an early dinner somewhere?"

She looks out the window, where the blizzard is raging. "Do you think your plane will really take off?" She sounds both hopeful and fearful. "It's a real Michigan night." Her tone turns apologetic, as if she is afraid she's disappointing me. "I don't really feel like going out in all that. Why don't I just heat up a couple of Lean Cuisines in the microwave?"

I nod my assent, uncomfortably aware of the time passing. She gets up, gathers the cards into their pack before she asks, "You're done with these, aren't you?" I nod again. She returns them to their place in the bureau drawer on her way to the kitchen. I hear her opening the freezer.

"Where's the phone?" I want to know.

"It's in the bedroom. You'll see it. Don't you want to call Derek?" Derek was a friend of mine in high school, someone I haven't seen since I moved away. My mother's run into him with his family a couple of times at the mall. "Or Elsa? She'll never forgive me if she hears you were in town and didn't call her." Elsa is my aunt, her sister.

"I'm just going to call the airlines and see if my plane is still taking off tonight." I wish I could keep the testiness out of my voice.

I step into her bedroom and am struck by the familiar scent of White Shoulders, the perfume my mother has always worn. Most of the furniture is the same as it was in the house I grew up in—the bed frame, the dresser, the dressing table. Missing is the large armoire that my father built, that housed his things.

I sit on the new rose-colored comforter. It's stuffed with fiberfill, not down—my mother's cheapness again. The phone by the bed is a new thing; my father would never have put up with that. He had an inherent distrust of telephones—to him they were a vehicle for public, not private, communication. On the rare times he called me in California, probably not more than three times in the fifteen years I've lived there, he always delivered his message quickly, in a self-conscious truncated voice. And he always refused to leave a message if he got an answering machine.

An airline attendant with a flat Michigan accent informs me that the planes are flying, and on schedule. Looking outside at the blizzard I find this hard to believe, but I will it to be true. I glance at my watch—I should phone for a cab in about an hour.

I raise the window blind and press my nose to the cold glass. A circle of steam clouds the place where my nose has been. I trace a pattern into it, then watch it disappear as the steam evaporates.

Before leaving the bedroom, I stop to stare at a framed photo on the dressing table. It's a picture of my mother and father when they were in their early thirties, before I was born. She is sitting on his lap, her arms clasped around his neck. His head is thrown back. They are both laughing with abandon, in adoration, perhaps with lust. I never knew my parents like this but I love the photograph. I love knowing that for at least one moment in their lives they felt like this with each other.

Reluctantly, I go back to the living room. On the card table my mother has set out plates of bread; plastic containers of bean salad, coleslaw, cottage cheese; dishes of canned fruit in heavy syrup. The table is set and I stand there, not knowing what to do.

"Is your plane leaving?" she calls from the kitchen.

"Hard to believe, but they swear it's even on time. I should call a cab after we eat."

She sticks her head out of the kitchen. I'm struck by the mixture of regret and relief in her voice as she says, "It's too bad you're here such a short time. Are you sure you can't spend the night?"

I explain again about the clients I have to meet in L.A. in the morning. She bobs her head; she doesn't understand the laws of commerce, but she knows better than to think she can interrupt them.

"Go and wash your hands now. We're ready to eat." She shoos me toward the bathroom as the microwave begins to beep.

The liquid soap won't lather in my hands, as I rub them together under a trickle of warm water. I stare at my face in the bathroom mirror. The blonde profile, the tanned skin, the good haircut, all serve to hide the shadow that whispers in my veins.

Tell her, I say to the face in the mirror. Do what you've come to do. I nod in agreement, then turn to wipe my hands on the ridiculous tiny pink guest towels my mother has carefully displayed on the rack.

Ever the hostess, by mother has spooned everything from the Lean Cuisine trays onto plates, arranged it like a meal she has really cooked. The television is on again, this time with the sound.

"I hope you don't mind," she apologizes, indicating the screen. "I like to watch the news."

A man in a checkered suit so bad it's comic is drawing in chalk on a map—the local station here can't afford the fancy computer graphics that are routinely used to foretell the weather in L.A. He's chattering on about high-pressure systems, storms from the north, windchill factors.

I chew the bland food, better than airline food I have to admit, but only by degrees. My mother laughs at some joke made by the weatherman.

When the sports report comes on I think I have a chance to get her attention. "Mom?" I venture.

She turns to me, already anticipating what she thinks I'm going to say. She's out of her seat, saying, "You want more milk? Can I get you anything else? Are you ready for some coffee? I have a nice pumpkin pie and a Dutch apple from the store—I can heat them up for us?"

"Mom, please just sit down!" My voice is harsher than I mean it to be. "I have something to say to you."

An edge creeps over her face, but she sits as I've asked her to. The national news report has just begun, and I can feel her need to turn her attention there.

I once had to tell my mother about having broken the pocket watch that had belonged to her grandfather. I was about eight. It was real gold. She hadn't given me the watch yet; she told me she was keeping it for me until I was older and could appreciate its value. I kept taking it out to look at it and play with it until finally, somehow, I broke the crystal. I was sure it was irreparable and I was torn with guilt over destroying something that was precious to my mother. I didn't sleep the whole night before and when I finally told her, I cried. She was extremely kind. She said the watch could be fixed and that as soon as it was she would give it to me, since I had obviously learned to appreciate its worth.

When I was nineteen I was madly in love with Michael, a boy I'd met at college, and I expected her to share my elation. She instead responded that she was sickened, she hadn't raised me to be "that way," she was ashamed to call me her son.

After Robert died last year I called to tell her. "I don't know what to say," she said. "I don't understand, but I'm sorry if you hurt."

She sits before me now, her brown eyes cloudy behind her glasses. Her cheeks are soft and lined and tinged with rouge; her permed hair frizzes gently over her forehead. She still goes every two weeks to the beauty parlor, has it tinted a light brown.

She is my mother. She is seventy-one. Her husband is dead and she has one child, who lives in California. I think of all the ways we are known to each other, all the ways in which we are unknown.

Bravely, she speaks first. "What is it, Greg? What is it you want to tell me?" I see in her face a determination to hear whatever it is, and I love her fiercely for this.

I open my mouth, but the words that follow take me by surprise. "I want you to come to California. I want you to come and stay with me. I'll send you a ticket."

This is not what she expected either, whatever that might have been. She relaxes a little while she demurs. She's afraid to fly, especially with all the things that have been happening lately, the plane crashes, the hijackings. She sees them on the news. And she can't get away. She has her doctors' appointments. She helps Lenore out by watching the baby a few times a week. And what would she do in California anyway? She'd just be in the way.

"No," I contradict her, growing more insistent. "You should come right away. Get out of this winter! Come see my house! We'll go shopping! I'll send you a ticket this week!" I am seized with urgency.

She's overwhelmed. It's been years since I demanded anything of her. For this reason, more than any other, she agrees.

"I guess I could take a couple of weeks. But not next week— I get my hair done next week. I'll come the week after that." Her head is already full of plans: cancel the newspaper; get Mrs. Fletcher across the hall to bring in the mail; use up the food in the refrigerator so it doesn't go bad.

I sit back in my father's chair, full of surprise and accomplishment, though this is not what I had intended to accomplish. My news seems less important, somehow, than this plan.

I see it is time for me to start out for the airport. I go into the next room and call for a cab. Peering out the window I see that the snow has stopped, and the night beyond is cold and blue. Perhaps they'll have the runways cleared after all.

As I wait for the cab I help her wash the supper dishes. She washes, I dry and put away, just like when I was a kid. In what seems a very short time I hear the beep of a horn and see from the window a pair of headlights in the driveway below.

My coat is toasty from the heating vent where it's been drying all afternoon. My shoes are mottled, stiff and uncomfortable as I slip them on.

"Remember," I say as I give her a quick embrace, "I'm taking you shopping at Neiman Marcus." She giggles like a girl, and I shut the door behind me.

Joyce Thompson

This kid looks like a perfect cross between my son and my daughter, which makes a certain amount of genetic sense. I do remember the hat; I could never wear it when we went to visit Great Aunt Kate, who belonged to the Audubon Society and strongly believed that God's creatures were not put on earth to become accessories. I personally adored the feather, which was very soft.

Joyce Thompson is the author of five novels: *The Blue Chair, Hothouse, Merry Go-Round, Conscience Place,* and *Bones.* She has also written two collections of short fiction: *35-Cent Thrills* and *East Is West of Here.* Thompson teaches fiction workshops at universities and writing conferences throughout the West.

Thompson, who lives on an island in Puget Sound, is presently working on another novel, *Paradise Illustrated.*

JOYCE THOMPSON
First Day of School

Take it easy, kid, the cop said, but Chuckie couldn't take it easy right then. The cop wasn't much older than him but he was dressed, covered up, while all Chuckie had on was cutoffs. No shoes, no underwear. The second cop was staring at his tattoo, not the way women did, and Lorena was staring out through a slit in the polyester drapes, one eye purpling, wearing his T-shirt which was big enough on her to hide her snatch. A foot down lower Tiffany, Lorena's kid, stared too. One side of her hair was braided and the other half hung loose over one shoulder.

The cop reached for Chuckie's arm, but Chuckie danced away. Keep your hands off me, asshole, Chuckie said.

While he was dodging the first cop, the second one got hold of his forearm. When Chuckie tried to pull away, the cop leveraged his arm behind his back, not hard enough it did hurt but so it could. The first cop moved in slow and cautious, which gave Chuckie time to swing. His arm hit the first cop full in the chest, so that he stumbled back a step or two and Chuckie felt a rush, a little hit of victory, until the second cop yanked his arm so high and hard Chuckie could have scratched the back of his neck.

Static and a woman's monotone kept spitting out of the walkie-talkie on the first cop's belt. It reminded Chuckie of Lorena's bitch bitch bitching and it made him mad. He raised his knee and aimed it at the first cop's balls but hit his belt buckle instead. The asshole moved around and grabbed his other arm. You're right next door to resisting arrest, buddy, the asshole said.

Chuckie looked back to the window in time to see Lorena step away from it, and the drapes fell closed, hiding the kid's body while her serious little face still stared, and once she knew her mother wouldn't see, Tiffany opened up her pouty little mouth and stuck out her tongue at him. Chuckie kicked but couldn't reach the glass. The first cop's fingers dug into his biceps and Chuckie could smell his after-shave, some cheap brand that old guys wear.

Guess you can see what she thinks of you, the second cop said. He laughed.

Fuckin' brat, Chuckie said. If it hadn't been for her.

The cops pulled him toward the stairs. Chuckie went but walked weird, smashing his hips against them, side to side, hoping that would make them let go of his arms. On the third step down, Chuckie jumped. His left ankle bone hit the metal lip of the fifth stair. The cops stumbled and recovered. Behind him, the second cop twisted Chuckie's arm.

Chuckie said, You bastards. My wallet's up there.

What else? the first cop said. Your stash?

No way. I want my wallet. I want my shoes.

Tough, the first cop said. You should have thought of that before you hit her.

Hit her? Chuckie said. Don't make me laugh.

Shut up, the first cop said.

A little black kid stood on the sidewalk, clutching a quart of milk. The chink who owned the corner food mart was standing outside the store, watching. Chuckie sent a wad of spit flying in his direction. The bastard wouldn't give you a pack of cigarettes if you were a nickel short. The cops walked Chuckie over to the back of their city cruiser.

Put your hands against the trunk and spread your legs.

No way, Chuckie said. He tried dancing some more, letting his legs lash out, so the cops were carrying his weight. They staggered. Pain shot through his twisted arm. Chuckie raised up both legs together, trying to bring the bastards down. They should have fallen but they didn't.

A hand grabbed Chuckie's hair and slammed his face down on the car. His nose flattened against metal and snot bubbled up. Chuckie rolled his head from side to side. The hand tightened and shoved until his teeth touched the gritty finish on the trunk. Another hand yanked his twisted arm until Chuckie thought it might come out of the socket. Fine. Then he could sue.

You are under arrest, a voice droned as he struggled. You have the right to remain silent...

Finally, with his face against the cop car, Chuckie relaxed. The bass beat from the radio of a passing car throbbed in his cheekbones. The walkie-talkie crackled. Through compressed nostrils, he took one deep breath and then another. When the fight went out of him, the hand on the back of his head gentled, just a little at first, then more and more and instead of listening to his rights, Chuckie remembered Mom, how when he was a kid and had a tantrum she held him so tight, squeezed and squeezed until he went all limp and calm and then she stroked his hair. Hands patted Chuckie's rump, felt in his pockets. By the time the Miranda business was over, the hand was gone and it was Chuckie who pressed his face against the car.

You can stand up now, a cop voice said.

Chuckie did, slowly. The cops stood with their knees bent, elbows, too, and tense, waiting to see what he'd do. Chuckie rubbed his shoulder, massaging the mermaid tattooed there. For a moment, they made a wary triangle, then one of the cops ducked forward, still eyeing Chuckie, to open the cruiser door.

Climb in, the cop said.

Chuckie climbed in, sucking in the cool, the static crackle, the smell of sweat and Naugahyde, blinded, for a moment, by the dimness after the bright morning sun. His bare thighs slicked over the seat.

Sit tight, the cop said. We're gonna talk to your girlfriend now.

The door slammed shut and Chuckie heard the click of four locks ticking, all at once. Outside, the cops in their blue uniforms took the steps two at a time, stiff and purposeful as those little action-figure cops he used to play with. They didn't look tired. Inside the cruiser, Chuckie was. The sludge of spent adrenaline ran thick in his veins and here, without a window open, he could smell the smell of last night's alcohol, that and the stink of fear, as they evaporated with his sweat. Funny, Lorena'd said he stank, but he couldn't smell himself then, only the musky odor of his wanting, and her perfume. The cotton in his head itched against the edges of his skull. For a moment, Chuckie wanted nothing more than to curl up on the black back seat and go to sleep.

Real men don't nap, he told himself, and he wasn't drunk enough to pass out, not drunk at all anymore but in that dry brown place that drinking leaves you when you stop, a thirsty place he didn't want to be.

He thought about Mom again, unexpectedly, and those little boxes of juice they used to take on picnics, thought about them so hard he could feel the cold hit his tongue from that first pull on the little plastic straw, about sandwiches in plastic baggies, and neatly folded paper napkins, Mom's wild hair and her brisk good humor, the boyfriends who all spoke more than one language. What was Lorena telling the cops?

He came home just as we were getting up, me and my daughter. School starts today. And he was stinko. There's a lot to do, first day of school. Tiffany, she wanted me to French-braid her hair. And I still had to make her lunch, peanut butter and jelly, that's her favorite, and do up all the buttons on her new shirt, and he comes in here like he's the head rooster or whatever they say and wants me to pay attention to him instead. Come on, there's time, he says. He grabs my wrist and starts pullin' me off to the bedroom. You can wait, I tell him. This is my baby's first day of school. Besides, you need a shower. That's what I said.

Mom smoothed his bangs sideways with a wet comb, then stood back to look him over. You look great, she said. Just like Peter Fonda. Now eat your eggs. I wonder who your teacher's going to be?

Well, I kept on braiding Tiffany's hair, but he wouldn't take no for an answer. First, he knocked the hairbrush out of my hand, then he swatted me on the butt with it. Big man, right? And right in front of my little girl. My girlfriends told me he was trouble, but did I listen? So Tiffany speaks up and says, Don't hit my mommy, or something like that, so he turns around and swats her and then I'm yelling at him, Don't you touch my kid.

Mom's hand was soft and cool around his hand. Chuckie was scared and excited. The closer they got to the school, the more kids there were. Too many kids. Mom said one of the good things about school besides learning was that you make new friends. He wished she'd walk him in and stay awhile, but she had to get out to the college for a nine o'clock class and she couldn't afford to miss her bus.

That really set him off. He started screamin' that I'm a bitch and callin' Tiffany a little cunt and all kinds of awful stuff. I mean, he can be nasty when he's drinking, but this was the worst. I told him to get out of our apartment and leave us alone.

From where he was standing at the bottom of the front steps, the school looked like the biggest building Chuckie'd ever seen. That big white ring around the door made it look like a big mouth that swallowed kids. They just kept marching up the steps and disappearing. Chuckie didn't want to get swallowed. He held on tight to Mom's hand.

He says, Your goddamn precious kid, that's all you ever think about. What about me? Huh? That's when he really started hitting me. He just kept hitting me and screamin', What about me? Tiffany locked herself up in the bathroom. It must have been the neighbors called you guys.

Mom crouched down short enough to kiss his cheek. While she was kissing him, she pulled her hand away and used it to ruffle up his hair. Brave boy, she said. You'll be just fine. I've got to run. Chuckie said, Mom..., but Mom was already running. He waited for her to stop and wave at him, but she didn't turn around. He watched her back until it disappeared around the corner of the school. His heart was beating so hard it hurt. Somewhere deep inside the school, a bell rang.

See here? I'm gonna be a mess of bruises. It's too late to put ice on this eye. He just went crazy, you know? And Tiffy with her hair half braided, she's gonna be late to school. Come here, baby. Mama's sorry. And on your first day, too.

Chuckie walked straight up the middle of the tall stone steps. He was a brave boy. Mom said. Right up the middle, into that big white mouth. He was standing on the threshold when the dogs came, three big bastard dogs running hell-bent down the hall, with some big fat guy running after them and yelling, Shoo! Scram! Get outta here!

In the frozen seconds before they hit him, Chuckie saw the dogs grin, their long tongues waggling. He could hear smell feel their hot breath, the clatter and scrape of their claws. Chuckie's lunch box went flying. So did his wind.

The fat man stopped running, planted his hands on his hips, panting, and watched the dogs retreat. Damn mutts think they own the place. He looked down at Chuckie. You okay, kid? Better hustle up. Last bell's about to ring. The fat man went back inside the school. Chuckie lay on his back and stared up at the September sky.

The cops unlocked the front doors and climbed into the car. The one who wasn't driving turned around and grinned at Chuckie. You're lookin' at first degree, kid. You did her pretty good.

Over his shoulder, the other cop said, And don't think about comin' back here, even if you do make bail. The little lady's gonna change the lock. He backed the car into the street, shifted, and turned toward downtown.

In the back seat, the wide turn rocked Chuckie against the door. Bail. Shit. He hoped it would be Mom who answered, not the new professor husband or worse yet, her new son. Peter wasn't a bad kid, really, except for being spoiled. You'd think he was made of glass or something, the way they treated him.

The cruiser stopped behind a yellow school bus loading kids. Even through the closed window, Chuckie could hear their shrill chatter. Back at the apartment, Lorena would be tying bows on Tiffany's braids, wriggling into her jeans, looking for the car keys. The bus driver shut the door and retracted the metal STOP flag, pulled into traffic. Of the waving mothers left on the curb with their bright smiles, two were frayed and dumpy. One was a babe, with big blonde hair like Lorena's.

The cruiser passed the school bus. Little kids in the windows pointed and stared. Chuckie leaned his head back against the seat and closed his eyes. He always hated school.

CAROLYN CHUTE
Maine novelist

Interview

by Barbara Stevens

*Carolyn Chute lives in
the Maine woods in a half-
shingled, half-tar-papered
cabin surrounded by broken-
down trucks, a cast-off wash-
ing machine, a snowblower,
and assorted plastic industrial
pails. Frantically yapping dogs
and honking geese penned behind chicken wire announce the
arrival of visitors. It was
"smoke-colored and cold" the
day I visited with Chute,*

Carolyn Chute

weather familiar to readers of Chute's two novels, **The Beans of
Egypt, Maine** *and* **Letourneau's Used Auto Parts.** *A fire
crackled in the wood stove, the house's only source of heat, and
beneath a cotton skirt, Chute wore pimply white long johns and
thick red wool socks. She clomped around the plywood floor in
worn leather shoes, filling drinking jars with water and stirring
the Campbell's Chicken & Stars that bubbled in a chipped enamel
soup pot. Over and over, she apologized for the meager Sunday*

dinner—or "dinnah"—saying it was the end of the month.

Chute has had the success most writers only dream of. Her first novel, The Beans, *which chronicled with fierce compassion the stark lives of Earlene and Beal Bean, took the literary world by storm. Critics compared her to Faulkner—whom she didn't read until after* The Beans *was published. ("His sentences run from here back to the airport. I couldn't make a sentence that long. I'd forget what the first part was.") Yet she and her husband, Michael, who has never learned to read or write, remain as poor as the backwoods folk she writes about. They built their modest home on seventeen acres in North Parsonsfield, Maine, with income from her books, but the money ran out. Field mice boldly scamper through the unfinished, insulation-pink walls, nesting in the cupboards and feasting on dog food. The Chutes have no television or telephone. The bathroom is an outhouse.*

Chute grew up in a working-class family in Cape Elizabeth, Maine. She hated school, and at sixteen she dropped out to have a baby and get married. Divorced eight years later, she took on a series of low-paying jobs to support her daughter—canning chicken, picking potatoes, scrubbing hospital floors. It was then, she says, that she learned firsthand about poverty. Having acquired her high school diploma during her first marriage, she took college courses here and there when funds were available. Eventually, she wound up working as a correspondent and columnist for the Portland Evening Express. *About ten years ago, her second child, a boy, died at birth. After this devastating experience, Chute threw herself with renewed vigor into her writing.*

The room she writes in is crammed with four large worktables, stacks of apple boxes—stuffed with reference books, letters, scrapbooks, old journals, and office supplies—boxes of Christmas decorations, Halloween costumes, Easter baskets, and Easter grass. Among the many assorted items tacked on the walls are a raggedy state of Maine flag and a photo of some red Durham oxen. (Someday, she and Michael would like to own a pair.)

At present, she's at work on a soon-to-be-completed third novel, hunting and pecking on her new electric typewriter. (Both The Beans *and* Letourneau's *were written on a hand-me-down manual with missing vowels.) Now and then she'll move from her desk to an old upholstered rocker. She sits there and sketches, drawing the faces of her characters or arrows pointing from one relationship to another, mapping out the plot. She works between eight and eleven hours a day, fueled by buckets of Red Rose tea flavored with honey and milk.*

STEVENS: *You're working on your third novel, is that right?*

CHUTE: I'm contracted to get it done in a year. I wish I had five years.

Can you talk about it?

Right now, I'm calling it *Merry Men*, and my editor likes the title. As in Robin Hood and his merry men, and it's kind of like that. A guy who's poor who robs from the rich. Mostly, what he does is he gives things away and plays tricks on the rich people. The one he tortures the most is his own brother, who's rich. That's basically what it's all about.

How is it coming?

Kind of along the same pattern as *Letourneau's*. Real slow and painful. But I'm patient with it. This is the one difference. I saw that *Letourneau's* worked out in the end, and I have faith this one will too. It just looks like junk right now. But I know in the end I'll be satisfied with it...I hope. I'm trying to be optimistic.

Do you mean with The Beans *it was different? Did that come more easily?*

Well, I was looking at it the other day. No wonder it came more easily. It's a piece of junk. I wish it would disappear off the face of the earth. Oh my God, what a crummy book. I really am awful embarrassed.

You really feel that way?

I didn't say the things the way I wished I could have said them. And those little sentences are so...babyish. These ladies down the road were interviewed once about what it was like having a writer living up the road, and they said they thought *The Beans* was like a book written by a school kid as a homework assignment. At the time I thought, those creeps! Now I think they were right.

Is that because you feel you've grown so much as a writer?

I hope. I hope. I hope. My students are so anxious to get published. I say, "Don't get too anxious, because once it's in print, it's in print forever." It's almost better to wait awhile. But then again, when you get published, it is so rewarding and inspiring that you want to work more. So in a way, it's good, and in a way, it's bad.

Do you still teach?

I probably all my life will teach once in a while. I've been teaching at the Stone Coast Writer's Conference in Gorham [Maine]. That's, like, for one more year, I hope. It's during the summer, and I don't do too well in the heat, so I'd just as soon see the end of that.

Does teaching help you with writing? Or does it make it harder?

It's harder. For one thing, it generates a lot more mail because your students will write. The other thing is you're way out of your workroom. You're into the world. You can't make up life if you're living life. But sometimes it's good to get a refreshing change, you know, like if you're between books, or even *in* a book, once it's going. One of the things I like about a two-week conference is that when you're working on a novel, which takes three or four years to work on, you have no sense of completion. It's, like, never done. Whereas with a two-week conference, you have the sense that you accomplished something.

When you're writing, do you ever get to the point where you get stuck, and it just dies on you?

Yeah, most of the time.

What do you do?

Just keep hitting my head against the wall. I put in between eight and eleven hours every day—even the weekends, if no one comes. So something is bound to happen.

What do you do when you're sitting there for eight hours and it's not coming and you're stuck?

I do try to find a lot of excuses when it's going bad not to go there and do it. But then the time comes when you gotta sit there and I just keep starting over when it doesn't seem to go well. I probably do that too much.

You go back to the beginning?

Not necessarily the beginning. There's no actual beginning and end in my work until the last few months. There are no actual pages. I don't even number them. If someone asked how far along am I in my novel, I could not even say I even have one finished paragraph.

It's sort of like deer hunting. You spend a lot of time running around the woods wasting your time. You might go out there for ten years and never get a shot off. You might get a shot and miss. More likely, you just blow a deer's jaw off, or a foot. Then you can't find the deer. You hunt for years, just maiming deer. Shooting at a rototiller. A few picnic tables. A woman wearing white mittens. Eventually, all at once, all in one moment, you kill a deer and bring him or her home. That's the way it is for me writing a book. A lot of mess and weirdness, then all at once, I bag it…all in a few weeks. Bang!

How do ideas come to you? Is it a character? Do you get captivated by an idea, a scene, a personal experience?

When I work I sort of go into a very quiet, almost meditative state, not dreamy, but kind of. So probably no ideas are involved. It almost feels sometimes like you're psychic, like you're pulling in something that already exists. It feels like that.

I feel that the best fiction that comes from us comes from our subconscious. It comes from associations, and it comes from moments in your life that were highly dramatic. I think that's what we tend to work on all the time, these little highly dramatic moments that really touch us.

50

How do you get yourself in that state?

First of all, I can't have, like, dentist's appointments or anything—for *months*. I have to know that I have a big block of time to myself. I can't have plans to go anywhere. Like I have to go to Baltimore next week, and I find it very distracting. It's very threatening to me to travel. I'm that kind of person. It's probably more disruptive to me than it might be to someone else.

You need to know you have a big block of time? What else do you need?

Quiet. No responsibilities.

Is this one of the reasons you don't have a telephone?

Oh yeah. And all the mail is very disruptive to me. I have a lot of mail. I always think, I have to do the mail for a while. I could spend the whole day working on the mail. If I don't work on it for a day, then it backs up and I don't answer it, and then I'll go to a book-signing and some lady will go, You didn't answer my daughter's letter, and I'll go, Well, I know. I don't get to answer all my mail. I *mean* to. I may still. Even if she's nice about it, I know she's thinking, What a creep.

Do you have other little things you have to do? Do you have to write with a certain kind of pen or pencil, or use a certain kind of paper, anything like that?

I know what you mean about those little things. I'll go upstairs and I'll write in my journal for a few minutes, to get a sense of getting quiet. Maybe read one of my blurb books [publishers send her dozens of books in the hope that she'll pen some positive remarks to grace the dust jackets], and hopefully it's bad. I really mean it about that, too. If the book's bad, it helps. If it's good, oh, I'll be so depressed.

I love good books. I'm exhilarated by them. But not moments before working on a raw manuscript. Even my own finished work—it's not the greatest literature in the world, but it's finished—depresses me if I read it during my work time because the material I'm working on is so raw, so far from that. So hopeless-looking.

Then I work my way over to the desk. It depends. If things are going well, I bound over to the desk. If things are going bad, I kind of drag myself over.

What other things do you do to put yourself in trance? Is it just a question of getting yourself quiet?

Oh, here's the other thing. Quiet—but *fast.* Caffeine. I definitely need caffeine.

Once I went to a University of New Hampshire poetry and fiction reading, quite a long time ago. I had never had anything published except for [a poem] in a college—what do you call it—quarterly. And these were all published writers, these people reading, Real Writers, you know. And so my friend, she was a newspaper writer, and myself, and this guy who was going to read the poetry, we all went down and afterward we went to a barroom where they were all going to spend the rest of the evening. We sat in a booth right behind these Real Writers, and cocked our ears and listened to what they had to say. Not much very important was said for quite a long time. Then, eventually we got to the real meat of what we wanted to hear there. One of the writers said, "I never would have published if it weren't for coffee."

Well, I went home and got myself a can. I don't know, I might have gone into tea first. Yup, I tried tea. Did tea for quite a while. Then I went to coffee because I found it was a little more powerful, but then it was too powerful. You know, it kind of eats your insides up. So I'm back on tea now. It's true. Coffee, yeah, it makes you very...creative.

Does it make you write fast?

Yeah. I find that caffeine has a certain amount of time. I try not to start before nine o'clock because I have good energy in the morning and I don't want to waste that. I need caffeine for the afternoon. So I start around nine o'clock, and by one o'clock it's starting to cook. And then you get over that little slump in the afternoon, and by three o'clock, vrroomm. So I have that good caffeine time probably until about seven and then you just sort of crash, and I don't mean that I get down, but I get very wiped-out feeling. You feel exhausted. And that's from caffeine. I know, it's just wore you out. But I have, like, four hours of really perfect writing time. Not only that, but I've had the quietness before that. It's a real science, you know.

Do you write short stories anymore?

No. I don't like giving up my characters in such short amounts of time.

Is it easy for you to get inside the heads of your characters?

Once I've got them together. Those last few months I find myself so immersed in that world that even Michael joins me, and we start talking about them and stuff.

Because it's so real?

Yeah.

But how do you get to the point where it's real?

I don't know. I don't know how I finally get there.

Is it hard?

Yeah. It's awful. It's so frustrating.

Are they as real to you as real people?

In the end. In the end. But not for a long time. Right now they're not too real. Kind of like shadows. It's awful.

So you're a big rewriter then?

Oh, it's all rewrite. I feel like a lot of time my writing is like having about twenty boxes of Christmas decorations. But no tree. You're going, Where do I put this? Then they go, Okay, you can have a tree, but we'll blindfold you and you gotta cut it down with a spoon.

Do you ever think to yourself, Why am I doing this?

Why am I doing it? Because I can't do anything else.

On my bulletin board I have a Kurt Vonnegut quote. It sometimes makes me feel a little bit better. He says, "When I write, I feel like an armless legless man with a crayon in his mouth."

That's it! That's it. That's great.

People think you just sit down and whip things off. My ex-husband's wife said to my daughter, "Well, your mother can help you out, because she just *came* by that money. Your father and I have to *work* for a living." I just came by that money! I worked for years for no pay. I work all the time. Except now I do get this monthly amount from the publishers.

From your earlier books?

No. For the one I'm working on now.

Doesn't money still come in on the others?

No, because they gave me such huge advances.

People think best-selling authors are rich. Why aren't you rich?

The IRS takes thirty percent. You take fifteen years of no pay to write a book. You get paid all at once and the IRS considers it a windfall profit. Also, it's our sole income, almost.

Did I hear that someone bought the movie rights to The Beans?

I hope they never do that movie. I did want them to do it, but now that I've seen the script, I'm a little disappointed. There's incest everywhere. He added incest where reviewers didn't even see incest. *The Brady Bunch Goes Incestuous.*

I heard it's on, though. They're still trying to get the money together. But nobody wants to finance it. I know one outfit said they don't want to do it. They already did *The Color Purple* and they don't want to do another poor people's story.

There's a lot of anger in your work, but it doesn't leap off the page. You mix it with humor, and there's so much compassion and love in it, yet I feel that the person who is writing it is angry.

That's the difference between literature and writing an essay. If I write essays, they tend to be very angry and very bitter and very negative. I've got one now I'm doing with *Esquire*. They said, "Do the article on why America hates the poor. And do it with some speculation on things and a little bit of personal experience." Well, boy, I ripped into *that*. Then they said,

"We'd like it to be a little more personal and a little *less* speculation. So if you could rewrite it, try to make it, you know, like *The Beans.*" Well, if they wanted fiction why didn't they tell me that to begin with? I was disappointed, because here was my chance to get *mad.* Because when I do my fiction I can't do that.

In the article you wrote recently for Mirabella *[about the yuppification of Maine], you were angry there.*

Yeah.

But you temper it.

The reason why I'm angry is because there is so much at stake that's beautiful. That's why I'm angry. I wouldn't be angry if everything was crap. I'd say, Oh, well. I'd give up and lie down and die. There is so much beauty that's at stake, and I want to show—even in the essays—that that's *why* I'm angry. Not only that, if you just rage on and on, no one's going to listen to you.

Also, I find humor and seriousness, beauty and ugliness, make each one more powerful when you juxtapose them. Like, if you have [she drops her voice] *seriousness* and then humor, you laugh all the harder because you've been so serious, and then it goes back to serious, kind of jerks you back there again. It's sort of like going back out into the cold, and then you come into the heat. And the same with ugliness and beauty. You take them and juxtapose them, and they're both twice as striking. In an essay I do get a chance to express all that more.

Is that fun?

Yeah, because in the fiction you have to create characters to be living beings. It's like being God. You can't mess with them. You have to let them develop and become what they want to be. If you don't approve of something, you've got to let them do it, whether you like it or not. In an essay, it's you. Even though in fiction little bits of yourself come through, it's not consciously yourself.

Do you consider your work autobiographical?

I've heard people say, Oh, the first novel of every writer is autobiographical. I can't imagine that. I've even tried. I've tried doing that in the novel I'm working on now. I tried to write about a person I was close to, and it seemed to just fall apart.

How did you recognize what was unique in your own work and once you recognized it, how did you develop it?

The first Stone Coast Conference was ten years ago and I went to that—not as a student, but as a hang-around person. I was at a reading and there was a guy there who was doing a reading, a novelist. I don't remember who he was, but I remember he was good. He looked like a novelist. He had the tweed jacket and everything—gray hair, a beard. Anyway, he read, and I thought, My gosh [her voice goes soft and sad], I could never write like that. I will never be a writer. I was so depressed. Because the way he wrote was, well, he made references to things I didn't know about, like Homer and things like that. He was a very academic kind of person. I thought, No one's going to want to read my stuff.

You were writing at that time?

Yeah. And later, during that same conference, I had a reading, where I got a lot of good feedback from some people.

Do you remember what you read?

A piece of junk. It was terrible. Terrible. But I thought it was great after people said that nice stuff, so it encouraged me.

So I began to think, maybe it's like apples and oranges. I mean that man had the tweed jacket and the grayish hair, he was taller than I was, his hair was shorter. He had a different face; he had a different thumbprint. I mean, he was a different person. His story is valid, but that doesn't mean that mine's not. I really, really around that time, came to terms with that, that you don't have to copy other people or even ever try. You just bring yourself to your fullest, whatever that is.

Did you always have your own style?

Maybe I kind of did. And I think partly here's one of the reasons: I have learning disabilities. I have a lot of learning disabilities. I have a real problem with memory. I have a real bad problem with...word recall. And as I work, I can't even hang on to a thought. It's just gone. Some people say, Oh, that's because you're a Gemini, but I just have a real struggle when I work and I think I've had to work around those disabilities somehow and develop what I could do, and what I could do was work with dramatic situations because I did have a lot of mess in my life, dramatic kind of things.

I am a kind of dramatic person. I have very strong feelings about things. When I get mad I bust up the house. When I'm happy I'm dancing around the house, and everybody's got to hear about how happy I am. So when I work, I work around that drama, around that sense of everything being very deeply felt.

I write a lot of junk. On and on and on, all this junk. But every now and then this dramatic moment happens, so I lift that out and put that aside. And then I write all this junk: They're brushing their teeth, They're sitting there, They're looking around—you know. Then something will happen and I'll pull that out. Because those are the only strong things.

Do you just write and write and write, not even thinking about it that much, and then go back with your editor's eye and look at it?

Yeah. I love the editing part. I love the revision. I love all that stuff because once I've got the material, it's great, it's fun. The hard part is going after that Christmas tree with a spoon. Once you've got that Christmas tree home, the decorations go on.

What did you read when you were growing up?

I didn't read when I was growing up. My folks had TV. I guess as a kid what I did, which relates to my writing now, is the pretend stuff. I did all kinds of pretending. And, to me, that's even more important than reading. Because I think a lot of people read books, and they go, Oh, that would be a nice thing to write a book. But writing is not reading. It's not even the same thing. Writing is pretending.

I never made any conscious decision to write. I never dreamed of being a writer or anything. I didn't know books were written by people. I thought machines made them. I wanted to be a farmer's wife and have animals.

So there were no books that influenced you as a young person?

I did read a book once as a teenager, and I loved it. It's called *Seventeen* by Booth Tarkington. It's a sweet book, well written.

So that was the one book you remember reading?

That was the only one. I might have started to read *Red Badge of Courage*, but I didn't seem to get into that one. At school, they made you read that one. *Seventeen* I *chose* to read.

Who do you read now?

I don't have time to read much. I read so slow. And I read only a little bit before I go to bed. I don't really have much time for reading…because of work. So I don't get to read, really, what I want to read—often. Now and then I'll squeak one in there.

Why didn't you like school when you were a kid?

Three reasons: one, it was boring; two, I had learning disabilities, so some of it was hard; and third, the teachers treated you with disrespect. They would treat you like they expected you to do something wrong. They had rules that were silly, like you couldn't go to the bathroom unless you had a permission card. It was so military, I couldn't stand it. I was too shy to speak up in class. I never raised my hand—never, ever—or asked a question or answered one. So I might as well have not been there. I just learned I was nobody there. I hated it.

You left school to have a baby. You were young.

Sixteen. Boy, I figured a way to get out of there! Then when I got married, my husband at the time worked nights a lot. I would stay up all night and write my novels.

What were you writing then?

Junk novels.

Not something that got published?

Oh, no. I never tried publishing them. And I still wouldn't be published today if it weren't for Stone Coast Conference where people saw short stories I had and offered to publish them, then later, a friend, Madison Bell, helped me find an agent for *The Beans*. I never would have found one on my own. Some stuff in *Beans* evolved from those old practice novels of the sixties and seventies.

Do some parts of writing come easier for you than others?

None of it's easy.

I was just reading an interview with Eudora Welty in which she said that emotions were easy for her, to get down what a character was feeling, and so on. But what was hard for her was moving a character from room to room.

Yes!

Or having them do something like undress.

I have the exact same problem! I can't get them into another room, so I just make them appear there. Yes, and getting their clothes off. Absolutely. That is very difficult.

Do you listen to people talk a lot? Your dialogue is very—

Not enough. I talk too much. I wish I would listen better.

How do you decide whether to write in first person or third person? This is something I really struggle with sometimes.

I struggle with that too. I think I've given up on first person.

Why?

You can do almost all the same stuff with third person subjective that you can do with first person, but the thing is you can get a little bit fancier with the language with third person. First person really limits you in that anything a character wouldn't see you can't talk about, or it will sound too contrived. You're really limited. With the first person you have to enjoy using voice, but you have to have each voice different. I don't think I can work with first person anymore. Somehow I've lost it.

And sometimes I like to pull back and not see what's in characters' heads because sometimes it's even more powerful to just see the actions that they're doing.

You write in both past and present tenses. How do you decide which to use?

Past tense seems to give the reader the notice that the voice already knows something that is about to happen, and this builds a tension. Present tense means the voice doesn't know what's going on either, but there's an immediacy, which seems to bring the reader closer to the voice and the experience, but might sacrifice the tension which would have to be developed in other ways, such as a constant hammering, a rhythm of events, so that the reader expects something to happen again and again.

Your punctuation is distinctive—lots of ellipses with extra space between the dots, and capitalized words. Was this something you deliberately developed?

Ellipses give me the feel of poetic space, a pause which I prefer at times to just a comma. I want a more visual pause, so that words or groups of words float on little islands, like in poetry. Extra space between the dots? I guess there is. I didn't realize that before, but I guess so. I still use words in caps sometimes but not as much. That's one of the things I would change in *The Beans*.

Who's your editor?

Cork Smith. If Cork either dies or quits the business, I am quitting. I am never working with anyone else. I know I get fixed on people but I have heard lots of horror stories about other editors. I've never heard of any editors who do what he does. First of all, he's not a writer, he's never been a writer. He is an editor. And he sits down with you and it's like you almost...merge somehow. He's left-handed, so you sit at the desk together like that real close, and it feels like you're the same person. And if there is something he feels isn't right about it, it's almost as if you really already had that in your subconscious, and he just sort of got there first.

Do you feel that people who don't write don't understand what you do?

Yeah, but I don't understand electricians either, but you

know they're nice people. You have other things in common, though, life. And a writer really writes about life, so to really write about life you gotta kind of get in it, I guess. I know what you mean, though. They don't.

Do you ever get hungry to talk about writing?

Yeah, that's what the conferences and all that stuff are for. But, also, Michael understands. Because he has to hear it so much and he's so close to me that he knows. I talk about it with him constantly.

You talk about the characters in your books, and what's going on?

Yeah.

Does he help? What kinds of things does he do to help?

He'll say, I just saw Blackstone [a character in *Letourneau's*] in town; he was doing this and this and this. And I'll go, Wow, that's great!

What he'll do a lot of times is I'll tell him about characters and so he's on the lookout for them. So then he adds more to it.

Then does it feel more real to you because it's real to someone else?

Yeah, it gives you a chance to talk about it, and as you talk about it, you bring it out a little more freely than you might if you're sitting there taking yourself too seriously at the type-writer.

What was it like to be poor for so long and to write but never know if your writing was ever going to be read? What was it like to suddenly get published, to have someone say, We want to pay you for what you're doing. Was it just the best feeling?

Yeah. Yeah, it was. It was really neat. Especially when I got the check. It was good because we went out and got groceries, and I took a picture of all the groceries on the counter. It was so neat. First, before I cashed the check we took it over to [some friends], and they said Wow! And we all felt the check.

How has success changed your life? You said writing isn't as much fun?

I think that's partly because I'm more critical of it. If you're being critical, you're not being creative.

Do you get moody when your writing isn't going well?

You know how writing is, it's so…elusive. It's not like you get up and you do it. It's not like you're a carpenter, which can be very rewarding. You build it and it stays there. You know, it doesn't fall apart.

There's something really weird about writing. I wish there was something else I could do. I'm realizing I don't like writing. But I don't know what else I could do. Make papier-mâché dragons or something?

If I won the lottery I think I'd be a housewife. That's what I always really wanted to be. I just wouldn't have the TV.

What would you do?

I'd have my grandson over a lot. As soon as he got too big, I'd have other little kids over. I like little kids. I would cook more. I would maybe have a garden, and oh, all kinds of stuff. I would be busy all the time. Oh, I wish I didn't have to write. I hate writing. I hate it. I'm trapped in it now. But then, I try to think of all the other jobs I had, and I hated them worse.

BARBARA STEVENS lives in Rhode Island, where she works as a freelance writer, teacher, and copy editor. Her stories have been published in *Northeast* magazine, the *Atlantic*, and the *Emrys Journal*.

Siobhan Dowd, program director of PEN American Center's Freedom-to-Write Committee, writes this column regularly, alerting readers to the plight of writers around the world who deserve our awareness and our writing action.

Writer Detained: Thiagarajah Selvanithy
by Siobhan Dowd

*T*he war that has raged since 1983 between Sri Lanka's Sinhalese majority and its Tamil minority has cost countless lives—some estimate seventy-five thousand. The Liberation Tigers of Tamil Eelam (LTTE) have control of the island's northern Jaffna Peninsula; in the south, the ruling United National Party has declared a state of emergency under which people can be detained without charge or trial for eighteen months. This law is overtly employed as a bolster in the armed conflict, but it is also a

Thiagarajah Selvanithy ("Selvi")

useful method of silencing, often brutally, the many, and frequently armed, opposition groups, notably the extremist

Janatha Vimukthi Peramuna (JVP). The net result of all this violence, both state-sponsored and otherwise, is many additional thousands of deaths and disappearances, often involving the civilian population. In the late 1980s, it was hardly possible to drive from one city to another without seeing truncated bodies along the way. One Sinhalese exile—who left to avoid certain arrest after having unsuccessfully tried to help a friend escape—commented, while dwelling on the country's famous beauties: "Our sandy beaches are lined with coconut trees and are miles and miles long; they are really something. But no one uses them anymore. They do not want to be confronted with corpses each morning."

In this climate, it is, above all, the country's female population that has desperately tried to be a voice of reconciliation and peace. In the south, the mother of one of the country's "disappeared" journalists, Dr. Manorani Saravanamuttu, has formed the "Mothers' Front," which now contains some forty thousand women whose loved ones were abducted by one of the warring factions. In the north and east, at one time, there were two earlier "Mothers' Fronts," but these endeavors have only barely survived. The northern and eastern Fronts, though still extant, apparently now restrict their work to humanitarian relief. The southern Front is perpetually having to avoid being hijacked by political parties jealous of its popularity.

In 1989, a group of Tamil women proved successful in launching a fresh women's center in Jaffna, called Poorani, which had close ties to women's groups in the south. Its aim was to help the female victims of the conflict, many of whom had been raped. A young and gifted poet called Selvi, as Thiagarajah Selvanithy is known to her many friends, was involved in this group, and this fact and her outspokenness in her articles, poetry, and private conversations apparently led to her arrest in August 1991 at the hands of the Tamil Tigers.

Aged twenty-eight, Selvi has a brother and at least two sisters.

Her father reportedly either died or left many years ago, leaving her mother to bring up the entire family on her own. This she did, according to Selvi, with remarkable fortitude, running their chili farm some eighty miles south of Jaffna single-handedly. Selvi described her mother as a woman slight of stature whose orders to farmhands were nevertheless obeyed with alacrity.

When Selvi was in her early twenties, her own feistiness and belief in the separatist cause led her to join the People's Liberation Organization of Tamil Eelam, a Marxist group with strong links in her own rural district, Babuniya. However, she left the group in disillusionment when, racked with internecine disputes, it began to disintegrate. She decided to adopt a more peaceable life, took her advanced-level high school examinations, and entered Jaffna University's Department of Fine Arts, where she studied drama and theater. Had she not been arrested, she would have graduated this year.

It is remarkable that the university has been able to continue functioning at all. Few realize that Jaffna has had no electricity since July 1990 and no fuel supplies. Despite this, there are no fewer than four different newspapers printed by hand each day, on shopping bags, file covers, or anything else available. All the papers are tightly controlled by the LTTE, and their editors are routinely briefed by LTTE officials. No human-rights groups have been able to visit Jaffna recently, and the peninsula is virtually closed to foreigners in general. The people of Jaffna thus live in a climate of fear and isolation. Few dare to criticize the LTTE and most live in dread of an invasion from the south.

Selvi is unusual in that in private discussions she has been quick to criticize the LTTE for its harsh methods of dealing with opponents. She became prominent within the university when she helped found a feminist magazine called *Tholi* from 1985 to 1986. A member of the Women's Study Circle, she was also a tireless worker for Poorani, which LTTE officials are known to have distrusted. At the time of her arrest, she was producing two plays about the role of women in her people's struggle.

Selvi is also a poet who has shown promise of adding substantially to the rich Tamil literary tradition which, unfortunately, has been only rarely translated into English. The current generation of writers has largely fled the north. For instance, one famous poet now lives in Colombo; and two of three authors of an influential collection of political essays also left (one to Colombo, one to London) after the third was murdered. Selvi's poems, published in the Jaffna University's publication and in a local weekly called *Thisai,* not only lament the horrifying acts of carnage, but also examine the option of exile. Her conviction that she must stay in Jaffna despite the attendant dangers is most apparent in one poem, in which she addresses an absent lover, in exile in India: she admits that it would be soothing to be out of the fray, but fears that she would lose her sense of purpose were she to join him.

In May 1991, three Jaffna University students were arrested; Selvi's arrest, reportedly at the hands of the Tigers, followed three months later. One report suggests that a sister of Selvi's was allowed to visit her and another confirms that Selvi is at least alive. In 1992, a disturbing report suggested that she had been brought to a local hospital for treatment, possibly for her asthmatic condition. Since then, the only fresh news of Selvi has been that she is still detained. The Tamils do, apparently, operate a prison system of sorts in the north, though obviously the laws in effect in the rest of the island do not prevail here: thus, Selvi has neither been formally charged or tried, and the sole reason for her continuing detention is apparently that she was too outspoken, in conversation and in her writing, in her criticism of the Tamil Tigers.

Since the Sri Lankan authorities have no jurisdiction over the Tamils, readers may like to try writing to the American ambassador in Colombo, asking that all available efforts be made to indicate to the Tigers that Selvi's plight has aroused deep international concern:

Ambassador Marion V. Creekmore, Jr.
U.S. Embassy
210 Galle Road
Kollupitiya, Colombo 3
SRI LANKA

Ed Weyhing

I was born in Plasterco, Virginia, a gypsum-mining town in the Blue Ridge Mountains. I don't have very solid memories of this age, but I do remember my mother and father always being there and my older brother and sisters kind of spoiling me.

Ed Weyhing's stories or critical works appear in *Calliope* (Fall/Winter 1991), *Cimarron Review* (April 1990 and January 1992), the *Hollins Critic* (December 1990), the *Providence Journal Sunday Magazine* (August 1987), *Weber Studies* (Fall 1991), *Writers' Forum* (Fall 1990), and *How the Weather Was* (a fiction anthology from Ampersand Press, Fall 1990).

ED WEYHING
How Do You Know?

*W*hat if you hear something. What if you hear a child crying. Is it playing? Is it hurt? Is it afraid? Is it in trouble? How do you know?

Suppose there is a street, and houses, and driveways. The yards are wide. There are brick houses. The bricks are like red, except darker. The porches have screens and swings, and there are shadows, but there is white around the edge. There are trees. Some trees are called oak trees. And maple trees. Oak trees have acorns, which are something like nuts, and leaves with fingers. Maple trees have different leaves, not fingers—what do you call them? You shouldn't eat the acorns.

Sun is high up in the trees. Sun is on the roofs and the driveways. Sun stops at the end of the driveway. Then the street is almost dark, except where they took a tree away. They cut the tree up and a truck took it away. Sun comes through where they took the tree away.

People cut the grass and sweep. You have to sweep. The job isn't finished until you sweep. Some houses have white or purple flowers around the front steps. You call them "irises." Some have pink-and-blue flowers. What are they called? Something. In one yard a lady stuck bricks in the ground, around the flowers. The bricks are like red, except darker. In one driveway the man parked his camper. Some houses have fans in the windows. The curtains move. The curtains move, but the trees are very quiet.

On one house there is a ramp. The ramp goes from the front porch to a landing, then to the sidewalk.

Anyway, what if it is before lunch. Mostly it is quiet, except for a child on a tricycle. The tricycle has a bell on it. Mostly it is quiet, but sometimes you hear the bell.

Then you hear a car come up the street. The car stops. Maybe the car stops and parks along the street. Maybe the car stops *in* the street. Maybe the driver looks for a number. Maybe the car pulls into a driveway and stops. Maybe it is a neighbor's car. After the car stops, mostly it is quiet again.

Then what if you hear something. What if you hear a child

crying. Is it playing? Is it hurt? Is it afraid? Is it in trouble? How do you know? Are other children playing? Is the child alone? The child is not yours. Maybe you don't know the family. Maybe the child is only playing.

What if the child is crying again. Is it playing? Is it hurt? Is it afraid? Is it in trouble? How do you know? On television they tell children to cry. Holler and scream and cry, so someone will come.

Some children cry when they play. If the child is in trouble, it will go to its mother. The mother will know. Maybe the lady who stuck the bricks in the ground will know. Maybe no child is in trouble. Maybe the child is only playing.

What if you live on the street, in the house with the ramp. You live in the house with the ramp, and your friends live there, and the house mother lives there. You and your friends live there, and each morning except Saturday and Sunday you and your friends go on the bus to the workshop. At the workshop you and your friends fold yellow price sheets, and put them in envelopes, and put the stamps on straight.

Each morning you and your friends go on the bus to the workshop, except Saturday and Sunday. On Friday you get paid, and on Saturday you walk to the drugstore. It is only two blocks to the drugstore, one traffic light. Look both ways. Sometimes the white police car is there. If the policeman says to go, you can go.

On Saturday you walk to the drugstore and buy a candy bar. What is it called? It starts with a *B*. At the drugstore you eat the candy bar and look at magazines. Sometimes you buy a magazine with your money from the workshop. There is a magazine with cars. Once you bought the magazine with the swimming suit girls. You didn't show the swimming suit girls to the house mother.

Each morning you and your friends go on the bus to the

workshop, except Saturday and Sunday. In the summer, Wednesday is different. On Wednesday in the summer, you stay back and cut the grass at the house. It is your job to cut the grass and sweep. You don't like to sweep, but the job isn't finished until you sweep. Sweeping makes it look nice. The house mother tells you if you make the grass look nice she will get bricks to stick in the ground along the sidewalk. This is called a border.

What if you live in the house with the ramp, and it is Wednesday, and it is your job to cut the grass. It is before lunch. The sun is hot. There isn't any grape drink: that's only at night. You don't like to sweep, and you are edging the walk by the back porch. You think about your magazines, or about the bricks to make a border along the sidewalk.

Then a child is crying. You hear it crying, and you are edging the walk by the back porch. You hear it crying, and you are edging the walk and thinking about the bricks to stick in the ground to make a border along the sidewalk. You hear it crying, and the bell on the tricycle has stopped, and you remember being afraid. You hear the child crying, and you remember being afraid, and you go out front, and the child is across the street, and there is the car, and you go to her, and you are the only one. What if you are the only one to go to her.

What if you go, and you see her holding on to the tricycle, and crying, and you see the car, and the car door is open, and you are the only one. You see her, afraid of the car, and you remember being afraid, and you go up to her and put your arm around her. What if you put your arm around her, and the car drives away, and you are the only one. She is still afraid of the car. She is still crying. You are the only one, and you put both arms around her. You remember being afraid, and you hold your arms around her, and she stops crying.

What if her mother comes. What if the child's mother comes, finally, holding a towel around her head, and you remember being afraid, and you hold your arms around the child. What if the mother screams, and then the child is crying again.

Suppose there is a street, and houses. The mother holds her child. The child is crying. Other mothers come into the street. Grandmothers come into the street. Everybody is talking. Grandmothers come into the street and talk to the mother.

You live in the house with the ramp, and one of your friends comes out on the porch, and your house mother comes into the street and puts her hand on your arm. The white police car rolls up the street and stops, and the door opens.

What if you hear something. What if you hear a child crying. Is it playing? Is it hurt? Is it afraid? Is it in trouble? How do you know?

A. Manette Ansay

My brother and I were friendly children.

A. Manette Ansay's work has appeared in over twenty literary magazines, including the *Beloit Fiction Journal*, the *Crescent Review*, the *North American Review*, and *Quarterly West*. She has been a fellow at the MacDowell Colony, and recently won second place in the Editor's Choice Awards sponsored by *Columbia: A Magazine of Poetry and Prose*.

Ansay received her M.F.A. from Cornell, where she currently teaches creative writing by day and works on a novel by night. Next year she will be the George Bennett Fellow at Phillips Exeter Academy.

A. MANETTE ANSAY
The Wallet

*M*iller doesn't like these errands, but he can never find any reasonable excuse to say no. Today it's Band-Aids, like she's a kid or something, and can't just sop up the blood with a tissue like anyone else.

"Band-Aids?" he says, shrugging the phone against his ear. The cord sweeps a stack of papers off his desk, and when he stoops to pick them up he bangs his head. He doesn't like to be called at work; neither had she, for that matter, but now that she's home she calls almost every day. "You want me to make a special trip to the drugstore just for *Band-Aids?*"

But he can't refuse; after all, she isn't able to go and get them herself. Her feet have swollen into ghostly pale mushrooms, the kind that pop up all through the lawn after a good spring rain. And it had happened that fast: one day she came home from work and had to cut her feet out of her shoes.

He swallows the irritation in his voice.

"Fine, Band-Aids. Good," he says. "See you tonight." Then he stares at the paperwork flooding his desk, the numbers neat in their columns, crisp as ants.

After work, he phones Pete and says to cancel their court, Patty has to have a Band-Aid, immediately, it can't wait an hour for racquetball, she's cut herself slicing an egg.

"An egg?" Pete says. "Well, they're good for her, she should eat lots of eggs." Pete's first child is almost a year old, and he can still remember the importance of eggs. "Anything without alcohol or caffeine, she should have as much as she wants."

Glimmer Train Stories, Issue 4, Fall 1992
©1992 A. Manette Ansay

"She wants Band-Aids," says Miller. He thinks of her feet and feels ashamed. "I don't know what to do. She's having a really hard time."

Pete clucks his sympathy, but Miller knows that he won't cancel the court, he'll simply find someone else to play. Pete's wife went on a trip to Washington, D.C., just two weeks before their baby was born, tramping all over the capital city, her only complaint that she had to keep an eye open for places to pee.

"How's the baby?" Miller asks to be polite. He shifts from foot to foot as Pete lists her latest words: *carrot, sock, McDonald's*. He tells himself that, one year from now, he'll be talking about carrots just like Pete, but deep down he is afraid he is lacking something necessary, something normal men have that makes the prospect of a child a wonderful thing.

Miller never really noticed pregnant women before Patty herself got pregnant. Now he watches them in the bank, getting on buses, buying newspapers, bulky in awkwardly fitted business suits. At the drugstore, he holds the door for a pregnant woman he thinks is going inside.

"Oh, thank you," she says, embarrassed for him, and walks on. Miller stares after her. She's wearing low red pumps. Her feet are slim as a cat's.

The drugstore is crowded with gray-faced shoppers listlessly browsing the aisles. Miller grabs the first box of Band-Aids he sees, then steps into the checkout line snaking its way down aisle two. He feels it's unfair that he must wait in a fifteen-minute line for one little box of Band-Aids. He thinks about putting the Band-Aids back, telling Patty that he forgot. Instead, he goes to another register, hoping to entice a clerk into opening a second lane.

The wallet is lying there on the counter, well worn and smooth, vulnerable as an infant. It startles him; he blinks, as if he's just seen something he shouldn't. Then he slips it into his pocket, neatly, as though he'd been doing that sort of thing for years.

Good God, he thinks, *you've got to put that back*. But he doesn't put it back. He feels exhilarated. He sets the Band-Aids down on the counter and walks quickly out of the drugstore. With each step, the wallet bumps against his leg, a small persistent heartbeat.

His car is parked across the street. He whistles as he reaches into his pocket for the keys; his fingers stiffen as they brush the wallet, work their way around it. He hadn't meant to take it. He'd meant to pick it up, yes, but only to bring it to the checkout clerk, or even over to the pharmacist because the clerk hadn't looked reliable. Her hair was bleached white and spiked in random places on her head. She seemed like someone who would keep a lost wallet, instead of turning it over to the proper authorities.

He pulls out into traffic. Passing the drugstore, hunched down in his seat, he is amazed by the filth of the interior of his car. Snack-cake wrappers, Styrofoam coffee cups, and newspapers litter the floor. He can smell his gym bag yawning on the back seat, and beside it an assortment of sweat socks nestled in tight little balls like dung. His mood topples. He wonders if the past two years have been a terrible mistake: Patty, the promotion, this baby he somehow must love.

At home, there's a note on the counter from Patty with a lopsided smily face next to it. He doesn't read the note. He peeks into the den and sees one of her mushroom feet poking out from under the afghan on the couch. The foot makes him feel ill. It will be two more months before the baby's finally born, and as the due date gets closer, Patty talks about it more and more. She's excited about the baby, and Miller tries to be excited with her, even though what he feels is not excitement. Sometimes he studies her face, examining each familiar shape, each gentle line, but nothing he sees there reflects the slightest whisper of his own growing anxiety.

He sneaks guiltily past her and into the bedroom, where Frederick and Melissa are curled up on the bed. Frederick is a beagle-ish sort of dog, and Melissa an aging Siamese. Both are Patty's from when she was in high school. At night, they sleep crowded onto her side of the bed. Melissa slits her eyes, and a low vowel shivers in the back of her throat.

Miller takes out the wallet and opens it. Inside, there are credit cards, a driver's license, and a packet of photographs. There are three one-hundred-dollar bills, and some change. The name on the driver's license is Mark Daniel Frier. The face next to the name is an ordinary face; a face, Miller realizes, that's amazingly like his own. Nervous eyes. The beginnings of a double chin. Hair fading fast around the temples.

"Miller?" Patty calls, her voice thick with sleep.

He hears her struggle to her feet and lumber down the hall toward the bathroom. He puts the wallet back in his pocket, listens as she turns on the faucets. She does this out of courtesy because she knows how bad he feels when he hears her throwing up. The water runs for a long time. He waits for her in the hall, and when she comes out of the bathroom, her face is moist and red.

"Hi," he says, and moves to kiss her.

"Nuh-uh," she says. "I've got doggy breath."

She grins at him, and he is charmed. Her eyes are wide and pale and mysterious; she hasn't plucked her eyebrows in weeks, and they form blunt, muddy arches that almost meet over her nose. Her belly looks too-large and painful. He wishes he'd stopped and gotten her flowers in addition to the Band-Aids. Then he remembers he doesn't have the Band-Aids.

"You sick much today?" he says.

"Mm," she shrugs, "not really."

He knows she's lying, and he secretly wants her to lie. He doesn't like to think about the way she's spent her day: reading, watching TV, sleeping as much as possible, waiting the whole thing out. He doesn't like to think *This is my fault.*

"Were you able to keep down that egg?"

"What egg?" she says. "Oh, I gave it to Melissa."

She nibbles at the edge of her fingernail. "I don't know. I thought if I sliced it up like they do in restaurants I might want to eat it."

"I guess I forgot the Band-Aids."

"That's okay. It's not so bad of a cut, see?" She shows him her thumb, and he sees a light pink whisker that runs from the knuckle into the cuticle. It's fairly deep, and it makes him queasy. He cannot bear the thought of her being hurt. In their Future Family classes, he has to leave the room whenever the episiotomy is discussed. The other couples tease him; one of the women has bet Patty fifteen dollars that he'll faint at the first sign of labor. Patty laughed when she told him about this, and scratched between his shoulder blades the way she does for Frederick whenever he's startled or afraid.

At work the next day, Miller closes the door to his cubicle and fumbles the wallet out of his pocket. He checks around in the folds to see if he's missed anything. The phone rings, and he spends a tense five minutes arguing with someone's secretary about some figures he may have forgotten to send. While he talks, he flips through the packet of photographs. His favorite shows a freckled young woman eating a piece of white-frosted cake. She has the frosting smeared across her forehead and nose, and seems to think this is funny. Her belly is flat as a door.

In the afternoon, when Patty calls to ask him to bring home a bag of Cat Chow, Miller isn't the least bit annoyed. He plays with the wallet as he talks to her, re-counts the money, shuffles through the credit cards. He feels as if he is a wiser, calmer, more mature version of himself, the kind of man he imagines Mark Daniel Frier to be.

That night he rubs Patty's back for her, and her feet.

"You're sweet," she says. "You're so relaxed today. You're more like yourself than you've been since we got pregnant."

He kisses her on the nose. He is nothing like himself. He can't stop thinking about the wallet and wishes she'd go to bed.

"I think I'm going to bed," she says then, as if she's heard his thoughts. "You feel like coming too?"

He doesn't, but he gets undressed and lies down beside her, listening, counting the seconds between each shallow breath. In his mind, he plays with the packet of photographs, arranging them into a story. Three young men are scrambled together in a pile of autumn leaves. Jaunty plaid scarves coil around their necks, loosely, like colorful folds of skin. One of the men, Mark Daniel Frier, has a Nerf ball squashed in his hand. Time passes, the men are gone, and a woman is laughing with cake on her lips. More time; she poses beneath a tree in a long, red gown, grown older and serene.

Miller gets up and finds the wallet, which he's hidden in the toe of his shoe. He takes it into the kitchen and spreads the photos out on the table. He stares at the cake woman, hungrily. He traces the careless smiles of the men with his thumb. They are not smiling because they are supposed to. They are smiling because that's what they really feel.

The next day after work, he spends one hundred and fifty dollars of the original three hundred on a Burberry scarf, something he ordinarily would not wear. He doesn't wear it now, even though it is autumn and the scarf is a beautiful wool, and warm. He keeps it in his desk at the office; at odd moments in the day he reaches in to feel the dull rasp of the material between his fingers.

On Thursday he picks Patty up after work and drives her to
their Future Family class at the YWCA. He sits behind her on
a foam mat and counts as she breathes. All around them, other
pregnant women sit with their husbands; the room rustles with
their stertorous voices. The instructor talks about natural birth,
about breast feeding, about anesthesia. The word she uses is
choices.

"Aren't you afraid?" he blurts to Patty afterward, his breath
smoky in the night air. He's been thinking all evening that
natural childbirth seems so unnatural. Why have all that pain
when you can just take a shot?

"Sweetheart," she says, tucking her hand into the back of his
jeans. Her face is bloated, but peaceful. He is swept with a sudden
fear that she will die. And now, if she really does die, it will be
his fault for thinking it. He bites his lip, looks away, thankful that
Patty cannot read his mind.

The next day he takes the afternoon off and goes to the mall.
He looks at stereos and VCRs and color TVs. He finally selects
a Sony Discman, and when the salesperson asks, "How do you
wish to pay for that, sir?" he says, "Charge."

"I'll need some identification," the salesperson says. His front
teeth peek suspiciously from beneath his upper lip.

Miller says, "You have my credit card."

He has given him the Visa that belongs to Mark Daniel Frier.

"Some other form of ID. Something with a picture. A driver's
license, maybe?"

Miller hands him a driver's license. The salesperson studies it,
arches his wispy brows. "I'm sorry, sir, but is this a recent
photograph?"

"Never mind," Miller says. It's hopeless. He will never be
anything like Mark Daniel Frier. He snatches up the plastic cards
and stalks away. On his way home, he stops at a flower shop and
spends ninety dollars on red roses for Patty. Then he realizes this
will make her wonder why he suddenly has so much money to

spend on roses. One block from home, he shakes two out of the bunch and dumps the rest into the street. The buds look pale and worn against the asphalt. He imagines that, somewhere in the city, Mark Daniel Frier is giving roses to the cake woman, his wife, the mother of his beautiful children. She kisses him; they drink champagne. Classical music plays as he spins her in her long, red gown.

That night, Miller and Patty turn out the lights and watch TV. Patty's roses are in an orange-juice can on the coffee table because Miller nervously dropped the vase. She is lying full-length across the couch, and Miller has scooped her feet into his lap, rubbing what used to be her arches. Melissa and Frederick are tangled in the love seat, their limbs like the interlocking pieces of a puzzle.

"Let's pick a name," Patty says.

"I don't feel like it."

"You'd better feel like it soon," she says, "or I'll have to name it Mulligan."

Mulligan is her maiden name.

"Name it Mulligan, then," he says. He doesn't want to think about the birth; a child, his child, ripping its way into the world, Patty's hoarse, animal cries, like the ones of the women in the films they have seen in their Future Family classes. He stares at the TV.

"What's the matter with you?" Patty says. "Can't you be a little more enthusiastic?" She pulls her feet away. "*I'm* the one that's supposed to have moods."

"It was a bad idea," Miller says.

"What was a bad idea?"

Miller picks up the remote, changes channels.

"*What* was a bad idea?"

"Look," he says, "I have to tell you something." He tugs the wallet out of his pocket, clumsily tosses it to her.

"Miller?" She opens it uncertainly. He watches her face as her fingers scuttle around in it. "Who's Mark Frier?"

Miller changes channels again. A young man runs down a well-lit street and pauses by an alley, breathing hard. *Don't do it,* Miller thinks, but the young man doesn't listen, and ducks into the darkness.

"I don't know," he says.

Patty waits.

"I found it at the drugstore. I put it in my pocket and kept it."

He lifts her feet back into his lap and rubs at them harder, working his thumbs deep into the soles. Tears start wandering down his cheeks, one at a time.

"Can't you give it back?" she says.

He shakes his head. "I spent most of the money. I bought some things. Flowers." He feels foolish, and the tears abruptly stop. "I threw the flowers away."

"How much money?"

"Three hundred dollars."

"Well, we can't afford to replace it," Patty says, as though she's thinking out loud.

"I'm sorry."

"Miller," she says, and then, "Miller," again. "I don't know what to do." Her stomach bubbles upward as the baby shifts inside her, and he realizes for the first time how much she, too, is afraid. Suddenly, he cannot imagine ever wanting to be anyone but who he is now, sitting in this room, with this woman, his wife, holding her feet in his lap.

She is looking at him, waiting for him to speak, but he doesn't know what to say. Instead, he lifts her heavy feet to his lips and kisses them, one at a time. They grow limp, trusting their weight to his hands. He holds them there, suspended, thinking about the child, their child, and how it feels to be floating in darkness, mute, waiting for what you don't know.

Jack Holland

*This is a picture of my mother and me (at around age three)
in Dougal's Yard. I was actually a cheerful little chap,
though you wouldn't think so by the photograph. Perhaps I
was in a foul mood because I'd been told I wasn't to get a
ride 'round the Yard on my favorite carthorse. I can't guess
why my mother is so stormy looking—all my memories of
the Yard are happy ones. The conflicts came after I left it.*

Jack Holland was born in Belfast, Northern Ireland, in 1947. He graduated
with an honors degree in English from Trinity College, Dublin, and earned an
M.A. in theoretical linguistics in 1972 from the University of Essex, England.
After some time as a free-lance writer, he began working as the assistant editor
of Ireland's then-leading magazine, *Hibernia*. Holland left *Hibernia* to join the
BBC in 1976. After a year of television, he came to New York, where he
discovered himself a novelist—he has two published novels: *The Prisoner's Wife*
and *Druid Time*. A third novel, *The Fire Queen*, came out this June.

Holland has been a columnist for the *New York Irish Echo* since 1979, and, until
recently, he was the U. S. correspondent for the *Dublin Sunday Tribune*. Not
only has Holland contributed many articles to newsmagazines and authored
two nonfiction books, he has also completed two screenplays.

JACK HOLLAND
The Yard

*J*knelt at the side of the big bed where my grandfather lay dead, the rosary beads threaded through his pale, folded hands, his eyes shut, his head resting on a clean, white pillow. His cheeks sagged in as if molded around the high protruding cheekbones. The bones looked as though they were already poking through from under the skin, which was as cold and lifeless as the putty that Jimmy the carpenter used. I had touched the hands, and had recoiled at once from their curious cold lumpiness.

Uncle Ed was shaving at the mirror of the dressing cabinet next to the bed. He was stripped to the waist, his braces hanging down his legs and a white towel around his neck. He was of a lean and wiry build, with sinewy arms and neck; his shoulders sloped broadly down to the rounded, muscled tops of his arms. A bowl of water rested on the cabinet with a cup of shaving soap next to it. He was whipping up the soap into a lather with his fine-haired shaving brush, the handle of which was made of polished wood. The rather sickly odor of incense and the scent of clean linen which hung over Grandfather's body blended with the sweet soapy smell from Uncle Ed's lather. Church and barbershop seemed to meet in the bedroom.

I closed my eyes and joined my hands as tightly as I could. I squeezed them, being convinced that the firmness of my grip was the measure of the sincerity of my prayer. I still did not know many prayers nor to whom they should be addressed. I knew only of the sweetly smiling long-haired Jesus whose picture overhung my parents' bed and who I called the bearded lady. So all I could do was to ask Jesus to be nice to my granda. I repeated it over and over again with fervor until I judged that a decent interval had passed. Then I rose from my knees.

"Who'll feed the horses?" I asked my uncle, glancing out the window toward the stableyard where Duggan's Carting Company kept the big drays.

"Don't you worry about them," he answered; surrounded by the white froth of the shaving soap his lips seemed very red. "Mr. Duggan's found someone to take over when we go. Anyway, the horses won't be around here for long. Their time's up. It'll soon be all motors." There were already several shiny new trucks parked at the back of the Yard in a dark shed—a vile place, in the foul corners of which, among cobwebs sagging with dust and the shriveled corpses of flies and moths, lived hairy spiders. Smelly pools of thick, black oil gathered there and green globs of grease that looked like snot. It was strange, and repulsive, that these sleek new machines should accumulate such unfamiliar dirt.

In contrast, everything to do with the horses was nice to touch or smell or hear: the texture of their leather reins, the sound of the iron-rimmed cartwheels as they rolled over the cobblestones in Duggan's Yard, the jangle of the harness when they shook

86

their heads, the clop of their hooves, the reassuring munching noise they made when their noses were deep in the feed bags. There was even something pleasant about the sheer volume of their piss as it gushed out green, splashing on the cobblestones. Their dung, too, had a rich, cakey feel.

"What'll happen to the horses then?" I asked my uncle.

"Oh, they'll be put in a field full of nice juicy grass," he replied, carefully scraping one side of his chin with a bright silver razor; each time he completed one full stroke he rinsed the blade and the white blobs of foam now speckled with tiny bristles floated away in the bowl of water. He pulled down his top lip tightly across his upper teeth and with shorter, brisker strokes shaved the band of bristles from under his nose. Then he stretched his whole face and looked at it from various angles in the mirror, patting it here and there with the palm of his hand. Satisfied, he daubed it dry with the towel.

"But it'll rain on them," I asserted. Uncle Ed looked down and smiled, his face fresh, clean, radiant.

"You love them oul' horses, don't you! You're as bad as your granda. Sure, he thought of nothing else." Ed looked across at the corpse. "Horses were his life. Many's a time I saw him drag himself out of bed at three o'clock on a winter's morning, the rain lashing from the heavens, to go and tend a sick horse in the stables. I saw him stick his hand down the horse's throat to get it to take its pill."

I had accompanied him once, on a stormy night, when one of the horses had broken free and was roaming up and down the stables. We opened the stable door, carrying an oil lamp, and the yellow straw looked golden under its light. I stood back while he coaxed the great animal to come forward, then he seized it and led it quietly to its stall. It was dangerous work. His thigh bone had once been split by the kick of a horse's hoof. Now that he was dead, neither Ed nor Hugh, my father, wanted the bother of the job—though the fine old house we all lived in came with it.

"Will we be allowed to go to the field to see them?"

"You're moving to a new house with your ma and da," he told me, "and you won't have time to worry about the horses."

"But why can't I stay here with you and Granny?" I asked.

"Because we've to move, too," my uncle said, slapping some after-shave on his face. "It's a bloody nuisance, all right. Sometimes it makes me think I should've accepted Mr. Duggan's offer to take over as the caretaker."

I felt a sudden twinge of hope. "I'd help you!"

Uncle Ed crouched down on his hunkers beside me. "Aye, I know you would. But no, I'd have regretted it in the end, all the same. Having to be ready at all hours of the day and night—with no time to yourself in the evenings—always worrying." He took me by the shoulders. "The world's a big place—bigger than Duggan's Yard. A change'll be good for us all. Where you're going you'll have plenty of fun with your new friends. You'll have no time to think about this oul' place."

I had no idea where I was going, and the thought of it made me feel queasy. Where was there to go? Outside the Yard was May Street. If you went one way, you reached the docks where the ships lay berthed with their tall, colored funnels. The other way led to the great green dome of the City Hall, with its statues of bearded men and its grassy lawns. It was such a splendid building that the only person who was fit to live there was the queen of England. And if you went straight, you found yourself in the Markets, where my aunts lived. But the houses there were poor and crowded, with toilets in the alleyways that you had to share with the house next door. Nor was I tempted by the prospect of having more friends. I had one already who came to play with me in the Yard. He lived in a street at the back, next to the waste ground caused by a German bomb. The waste ground used to be a street. Opposite it was a sweetie shop. Sometimes my friend and I would go there to the old lady, who shoveled the sweets into long paper cones. We would talk about the bomb, and try to guess where the houses had stood. I told him that my grandfather and grandmother heard it explode, and how it scared the horses. Later, my uncle Ed and my father dug the bodies out of the rubble. My father said they were like burnt toast. Unfortunately, my friend never said much. He stuttered, and I got into trouble with my da for trying to imitate him. But I liked him well enough. Anyway, I had my pedal-car, and sometimes the carters would hoist me on the back of one of their horses and lead me 'round the Yard.

I blessed myself and hurried downstairs. It was strange to find the Yard, closed because of the death, as hushed and quiet as a Sunday but in midweek. The rain was standing in puddles between the cobblestones and in shallow little pools on the tops of the big barrels that were marshaled against the wall near the horse trough, row upon row, like great, dumpy soldiers. The puddles rippled in the cold February wind, which drove before it the little bits of straw floating on the stale water. The carts were covered with tarpaulin, their shafts lowered. My heart ached. There were days when I liked nothing better than to jump from barrel to barrel, or to hide in the hay shed, or to play Indian canoes with lengths of straw in the horse trough. Or on wet days I would set off in search of giant spiders in the shed at the back, or snuggle under the tarpaulin, pulled taut like a great tent across the carts to keep them dry. Best of all were the journeys with my grandfather to the stables, past the huge, hairy hooves and the bushy tails that went swish over the enormous haunches, sometimes flicking you as you went by. All the horses had to do was move: the floor creaked and the walls trembled. It was as if they had the power to buckle the world into a different shape.

Now, I felt tight and uncomfortable in my new suit. All day

I had been forbidden to play.

Death had changed everything. My granny said that death was a woman dressed in black. Her head is always covered and bowed like a nun's, her eyes on the ground and her hands joined.

And like a nun, she walks so softly that she seems to glide over the ground. When she stops at your gate, you take sick. She steps through the gate, into the yard, and you grow sicker. As she

walks slowly toward your house, step by step, you become worse
and worse. Then, she puts her foot across the threshold, and goes
up the stairs, one by one. You do not hear her feet on the stairs,
nor do the stairs creak. But you know she is approaching. The
closer she comes, the sicker you are, until she reaches the
landing, and turns the knob on your bedroom door. She enters,
and raises her head. She looks at you, then reaches out her cold,
white hand with its long, skinny fingers. When they touch you,
you die. Even if you were as strong as my grandfather.

The gray, cold day had taken possession of everything. It was
worse than Sunday—muted, sad, endless. There was nothing to
do but wait until after the funeral, then maybe life would come
back. I went into the house. My da was sitting staring at the fire
with his hands locked together, his elbows resting on his knees.
My pedal-car was parked in the hallway. I looked at it, then at
him.

"Da," I said.

"Aye."

"Can I not play with the car outside after the funeral?"

He looked at me, his face red from the heat of the fire. "You
were told once, not 'til tomorrow. You have to learn to show
respect for the dead. Anyway, you can't get your new suit dirty.
Don't annoy me."

I touched its little steering wheel.

"What'd I tell you?" he snapped.

I pulled my hand away and went outside again.

Idly, my hands behind my back, I drifted across the desolate
Yard, listening to the sounds of the horses moving in the stables,
wishing I was up there with Granda again, helping him carry the
bucket of treacle to feed them. But I wasn't allowed to go up to
look at the horses now that I was wearing a good suit and new
shoes that were too tight. As I passed by, I was surprised to hear

the whir of a saw coming from Jimmy the carpenter's shop. Since the Yard was closed, and none of the men were at work, it was very odd. Had it been dark, I would have run back to the house, for then it could only have been a ghost. But seeing that it was broad daylight, I had no fear of going to investigate.

You had to go up the gangplank to get to his shop, which was next to the stables. Carefully avoiding the horse dung and damp straw, I made my way to the top. The shop was at the end of a passageway, and its door was wide open. Jimmy was there at his bench, and though he was dressed in his Sunday best, he was working the electric saw. A little cloud of powdered wood whirled around him; the same fine film that always covered his dungarees and turned his eyebrows white was now settling on his dark suit. But he still had his cap on, and as always, it was pulled down sharply until it almost covered one eye. He wore it that way to conceal the piece of shell that he had in his head from the wound he got in the First World War. Sometimes it made him act funny. But he was okay, and usually very friendly. Once, he'd given me a big red apple, and let me sit on the floor among his wood-shavings to eat it.

"Aye, you'll miss your granda," he said, switching off the blade and looking up at me. He grinned; his lips seemed pale because of the wood powder and his eyelashes and eyebrows were covered in it. "I'll make him the nicest cross you'll ever see. We always gave them a cross—no matter what. Your granda knew that. He saw it all as well. The Somme..." He paused and the strange smile left his face. I thought he was going to have one of his crying fits. But he didn't. He was thinking very hard. I wondered if he and my granda had fought in the same trench—the one where my granda told me they had to catch rats for food. "It's a dreadful thing for a body to lie in an unmarked grave. Come on in out of the cold and I'll show you." He switched on the blade again. It spun 'round so fast its edge was only a blur as it sliced through the long piece of wood. He beckoned me with his eyes. But I didn't want to go.

"I don't want to get my suit dirty," I shouted at the top of my voice. He smiled and nodded. I turned and went back down the gangplank and into the house where my da was still sitting by the fire. My granny was in the big armchair on the other side of the hearth. She was dressed in a black, crinkly-looking dress, with big shiny buttons. I went up to my da and tugged him by the shoulder.

"Jimmy the carpenter's started work," I said, "and he's wearing *his* good suit." He wrinkled his brows at me. "Can I not play in mine?"

"Don't you mind what Jimmy the carpenter does wee lad—his head's gone. He should be put away," my father retorted impatiently. "Locked up for his own sake."

"Jimmy means no harm, Hugh," my granny said with a sigh. "Sure, God love him, he's been through a lot." She looked over at me and smiled. "Aren't you the wee man in your suit." She summoned me over with a wave of her hand. Then she lifted me up and put me on her lap.

She always smelt of freshly baked bread, even when dressed up, unlike my mother, who smelt of perfume. Her hair was fine and white, swept back and kept in place by an old comb. She would hoist me on her knee any time at all, crush me against her breast and tell a story. It was nice and warm there, before the fire.

This time, she hugged me more tightly than usual, patting me on the knees as if she were keeping time to some slow, mournful song.

"Tell me about the time the fairies threw the coal at Granda," I asked her. She did not answer. I looked up. It was as if she hadn't heard me. She was staring into the flames of the fire, watching the sparks caught in the soft soot that lined the chimney's throat. "Granny," I said again.

"Go upstairs and see what's keeping your ma," my father said.

"Let him be, Hugh—he's doing no harm. He's just a bit restless. Anyway, Peggy's always slow to get ready. She's as bad as your brother Ed—faith, sometimes I think the two of them are better matched. There wouldn't be one always waitin' on the other." The bell at the gate rang. For a moment it seemed neither she nor my father had heard it. Then she said, "They're here." It was not like her voice, but flat and dry.

The gates were opened and the men in long, black coats and top hats carried the coffin through the small crowd of mourners gathered outside into the Yard. It was only when they lifted my granda out of the bed and put him into the coffin that Granny's eyes became moist, and she had to daub them with her handkerchief. My father stood close to her. She clutched his arm.

Uncle Ed and my father, along with two of the carters, linked arms and carried the coffin over the cobblestones, past the gangplank to the stables, toward the gate. My granny walked behind it, her daughters on either side of her. They were crying, but she wasn't. She simply looked up ahead of her at her two strong sons.

My mother and I sat in the back of a big black car. She was dressed in black, with a wide black hat and black gloves. Her dress only came to her knees, and when she crossed her legs it made a nice scratchy sound like paper crumpling. All the way to the graveyard she had her arm around me, her gloved fingers resting lightly on my shoulder.

Granny had wanted horses for the hearse, but Uncle Ed had said that horses were too old-fashioned. The hearse was a long car with a glass back so that you could see the coffin and all the wreaths laid upon it. We followed behind it, up May Street, past the City Hall, and then into a region of the city I had never seen before. There were streets and streets of small, red-brick houses like those in the Markets, full of menacing boys with dirty faces. After that, we could see green mountains above the rooftops, mountains I had never seen before. I wondered how long it would take to reach them. My mother said that it was too far to walk but maybe when I was bigger we could go there for a picnic.

"What's after them mountains?" I asked.

"Nuthin'."

"Nuthin'?"

"Nuthin' but an old bog and fields and more mountains," she said wearily, as if the world were too big for her. Perhaps it was— perhaps it was too big for all of us. Everything seemed so far from everything else. I nestled against her satiny dress. It tickled my face, and when I began to rub my cheek against her for a scratch she told me to stop.

The road got wider. There were lots of sweetie shops. We came to a wall with an iron fence through which graves could be seen.

"Is this the graveyard?" I asked. Mother shook her head.

"That's for Protestants." We drove past it and came to a big park with a river flowing through it and under the road. Tall trees grew everywhere, and on one side of the road opposite the park there was a glen with steep sides thick with bushes and trees. It was shady and dark. I could hear the river gurgling over the rocks. It seemed very far away. I shivered a little, thinking of how deep the glen must be. Then the car slowed. Just beyond a little lane-way, the gates of Milltown Cemetery came into view.

The burial hole was narrow and deep, its walls of damp, thick clay crumbling. My granny put her arm around me and pressed me against her hip as the men lowered the coffin down. I could see Jimmy the carpenter standing among the mourners, clutching his own wooden cross, the sweet-smelling dust from the wood still on his suit. My uncle Ed got clay on his shoes shoveling the first spadeful of brown, sticky earth into the grave. It clattered against the lid of the coffin. When it was over, the crowd broke up, except for Jimmy, who still stood with his cross waiting to stick it on the grave when the grave diggers had finished throwing on the clay. My granny told my father not to bother him.

Back home, a lot of the carters had gathered in the parlor. There was a small table on which sat a teapot and cups and plates with sandwiches, buns, and cakes. There were also a few bottles of black porter in the kitchen for the men who wanted to drink. Mr. Duggan, who owned the Yard, came too and stood by the fire for a while, warming his hands, saying a few words to my granny in a low, sympathetic voice. He wore a tight-fitting waistcoat with a watch on a silver chain, which he took out of his pocket and snapped open now and again. Then he went away.

I stood at the door or sat on the bonnet of my pedal-car. Every time a carter went by he would bend down and press a penny or a thrupenny bit into my palm saying, "Your granda loved you like you were his own son."

Every so often I'd glance into the parlor at my father to see what sort of mood he was in. But it was hard to tell with him. He might be smiling at somebody, or even laughing, yet when I said something to him, he'd start frowning. My new suit was hurting me, my feet were aching. And the afternoon was clearing up. Sunlight brightened the whitewashed walls of the old building that housed the hay shed.

I saw my granny go into the kitchen. I squeezed through the

guests and went in after her. The kitchen was full of men smoking and drinking with frothy mugs in their hands. The sour smell of porter hung in the air. I tugged at her elbow.

"There you are," she smiled.

"He's come for his pint," one of the men said.

"He knows where the best stuff is all right," another joked.

"Auck—leave 'im alone—if he's wise he won't touch that stuff," Granny said, standing between me and them.

"Can I change and play?" I said in a hushed voice without hesitating, as I was eager to be out of the kitchen as quickly as I could.

"Have you asked your da?" I shook my head guiltily, feeling like a coward. She looked down at me and smiled. "No matter—this once. It can do no harm. Off you go and I'll have a word with him."

I thanked her and left without looking at the drinkers, who seemed to be lapping up the creamy porter the way a cat laps up its milk.

Within a few minutes, I was changed. I hurried down the stairs and into the hallway, where the pedal-car was waiting. I guided it through the front door and climbed into the seat. My feet had barely touched the pedals when I saw my father standing in the hallway.

"What did I tell you?" he said with a scowl, coming toward me.

"My granny said—"

"Don't bring your granny into this. Get out of that car. And look at you—dressed like a ragpicker on this day of all days. Have you no respect at all? Is that oul' car all you think about? What will people think of us?" I bit my lip and stood up. He took me by the arm and gave me a tug as I stepped out of the car. My granny met us as we went back down the hallway.

"Sure, didn't I forget to mention to you I'd told him he could go and play—what with all the fuss here today. Leave him be. He's better off out there gettin' the fresh air than stuck inside with all that smoke."

"It doesn't show much respect for the dead," my father said.

My grandmother folded her arms, blocking our path. "And what do you think his grandfather would say if he were here today? Sure, wasn't it him bought him that wee car himself." My father looked from her to me, and relinquished his grip.

"Aye, right enough," he said softly, as if suddenly ashamed of something. Then, he crouched down beside me. "We'll be leaving here soon, son. And you'll have to face the big world outside the Yard. And you won't have your granny around to stand up for you. You'll have to fight for yourself, like I did."

I looked at him blankly. He talked of the world as if it were a boxing match.

"He'll be fine," Granny said.

"He'll have to learn there's more to the world than just pedaling around the Yard all day," Father added, standing up. "Anyway, off you go. And remember—you better get used to doing what I tell you."

I jumped in the pedal-car and took off up the pavement, pedaling furiously. I turned—the car went off the curb and onto the cobblestones, splashing through the puddles. I wanted to go harder and harder and not think about what my father had said. I swung the car around, bumped past the gangplank, and headed down the Yard toward the big gate. I was pedaling so fast it seemed I could crash through the gate and spring out into the street. But just before I reached it, I pulled up sharply, panting, my heart racing and pounding in my ears.

Beyond the closed gate, the traffic on May Street rumbled by. In spite of the strange solitude which had descended on the Yard, for everybody else it was an ordinary day of buses and trams and carts and bicycles. The big world that Uncle Ed spoke of was out there—the world with which my father threatened me. If I got down on my hands and knees and peered under the gate, I could see its feet passing by, and the wheels of its prams.

Eileen McGuire

*Aunt Mary took us downtown to meet the Easter Bunny,
who climbed out of an egg on the roof of the Scranton Dry
Goods store. When it was my turn to sit on his lap, I could
see the man's face through the gauzy black eyes of the
bunny head. This was unspeakably interesting to me.*

Eileen McGuire's stories have appeared in the anthology, *Delphinium Blossoms*,
and in the *American Literary Review*. She lives in Los Angeles and works in the
movie industry.

Eileen McGuire (signature)

EILEEN MCGUIRE
Inhale, Exhale

e've arranged to meet at Va Bene, the new Italian place on Melrose. Inching my way through Laurel Canyon in a lava flow of Friday evening traffic, I tune in to Dr. Penny Marcus to divert myself. A dirty little treat.

Dr. Penny, the three-minute psychologist, is counseling a caller named Donna, who only dates men she doesn't find attractive. When she likes them she gets too nervous, she says, and ends up doing something to scare them off.

I turn up the volume to savor Dr. Penny's solution.

"There's an old saying, Donna. If you can order dessert on the first date, there's no chemistry." The doctor allows herself a knowing chuckle.

"Oh, uh huh?" Donna says.

The psychologist adds that she once polled women of her acquaintance who'd had great success with men. What were their secrets? One woman said she took a lot of deep breaths when she was in male company. It induces a state of relaxation, says Dr. Penny, which is very important in attracting the opposite sex.

We think about it, Donna and I. Deep breaths, but no dessert. I used to make my boyfriend Patrick order the dessert so I wouldn't appear piggy. What did that signify, chemically speaking? Penny cuts to a commercial.

"If you are one of the single women who enjoyed Doctor Penny's last book, *Five Steps to a Lasting Relationship,* sign up for her two-day workshop April 15 and 16 at the Pasadena Hilton Hotel..."

One of the single women. Should I make a note of the dates before this red light changes? The driver behind me hits his horn and I'm jolted out of my trance. I punch another button on the car radio and welcome a bracing dose of rap music as I cross Santa Monica Boulevard. I'm ashamed of myself, thought I'd kicked the Dr. Penny habit at New Year's, when I also swore off browsing in the personal ads and self-help quizzes in *Glamour* magazine. By the time I find a parking space, I'm planning how I'll tell all this to Susan. "There should be support groups for people like me," I'll say. "People with psychological addictions to pop psychology."

I find her leaning against a protrusion of glass brick in front of the restaurant. It's one of those places where you sacrifice elbow room for the authenticity of their pizza oven. In a few weeks you won't be able to actually eat here; you'll just get to stand outside and watch other people eat.

"Hi. We're fourth on the list," she says.

Susan and I never hug or air-kiss the way people in L.A. do. We don't need to identify ourselves on the phone, unless I get her husband Henry on the line. Susan and I go back fourteen years, to a dorm room at Stanford. Tonight is the first night in I can't remember how long that we're having dinner without Henry.

"You're not in uniform," I tease her. When we all three meet on weeknights she's still in her lady lawyer clothes. Tonight it's sweats and one of Henry's tweed jackets.

"I didn't go in today," she says. "Off the beam."

"I have a Dr. Penny story."

"You broke down!"

As I repeat the consultation I heard on the radio (playing both parts rather well), Susan shakes her head, smiling. Her glasses could do with a good cleaning, I notice, and she's used an ordinary rubber band to pull a lock of her thick, straight hair into a Pebbles Flintstone topknot.

When I'm done she sighs, "Maybe I need to talk to Dr. Penny."

"You? About what?"

She scrunches up one side of her face, like a kid waiting for the penicillin shot. "I have to work up to it," she says.

On the phone this afternoon she said, "I need to talk," but I thought she meant "talk" in general—our fourteen-year ritual of conversation, always interesting, though indulged in less frequently since Susan got married.

This is news, I'm thinking as our name is called and we follow a hostess in a platinum brush cut to a marble table the size of a plant stand. Big news. Could it be that she and Henry are splitting up? I'm shocked at the little burst of pleasure that accompanies that thought.

I always pick the restaurant when we meet for dinner, usually a more obscure one than this, to broaden Henry's mind. Henry the Dull, Henry the Good.

Somehow it's always the three of us lining up at the movies, or bushwhacking through a new hiking trail in the Santa Monica Mountains. I struggle to find topics of mutual interest, and when I find one, like a shared appreciation of "Leave It to Beaver," we run it into the ground. I wonder why there aren't any "how-to" books to help people cope with the real problems, like what to say to their best friends' mates?

For a while we were an uneasy foursome, when I was accompanied by Patrick. The two men didn't like each other. They were opposites and recognized it, maybe enjoyed it. Around my boyfriend, Henry could appreciate his own solidity, his socially conscious career, his piece of real estate. And Patrick could complain all the way home about how boring the man was, or tell me how he'd shocked Henry with stories of his drug experiences, half of them invented for the occasion.

Now that I'm Susan's single friend, Henry wants to be my big brother, my confidant. At dinner he'll refer to some incident in my life, or a private joke, to show me how much Susan has told him, how he too can understand me now. I haven't spoken to Susan about it. She seems to think her husband and I are the best of friends.

Whatever Susan's news is, she's obviously not going to bring it up until after she studies the menu thoroughly. I eavesdrop on what sounds like a first-date conversation at the neighboring table. They're close enough for me to smell his cologne— Armani. He looks to be in his early thirties, a pixie in an oversized, expensive sweater. Long, restless hands. She's younger.

"Do you consider yourself an emotional person?" he asks.

"I don't really know."

Is there anything lonelier than a first date? I'm thinking, at the same time calculating the number of months it's been since I've had one. Seven months. I'm suddenly hungrier.

Susan puts her menu down.

"Henry working tonight?" I ask.

"Fund-raiser. Did I tell you he's volunteered for the Buddy Wong campaign?"

"No. Who's Buddy Wong?"

"Your councilman, Isabel."

"Oh yeah, I knew that. Why didn't you go?"

"We need a break from each other. It's been pretty intense."

"A fight?"

"Not exactly."

I am too tactful to ask what the fight was about. The waiter approaches and we order our calzones and rustic salads. At the next table the Inquisitor Date has moved on to other topics. We can't help but hear.

"What's your favorite ride at Disneyland?" he questions the girl.

"Mmmm, maybe Small World?"

"Small World," I mouth silently to Susan. She covers her face with one hand and rocks with laughter while I pretend to cough into my napkin.

Susan wipes her eyes. "God, I needed that," she says.

"So what was the fight about?"

Big sigh. The salads appear. Susan skewers a cube of Italian bread, a cherry tomato, than sets her fork down.

"I'm pregnant." She watches me closely as she says it.

"No. You're kidding!" She shakes her head, slowly, as it strikes me—Susan's child. I can picture her, dark-eyed and watchful, someone worth knowing. "It's the best news I've ever heard. How long? I mean, when?"

"October."

"A Libra."

"But here's the deal. The timing is really bad. Couldn't be worse. I got careless, maybe on purpose, I don't know. Henry . . ."

"Isn't ecstatic? What's his problem?"

"No. Look, it's not that he doesn't want children. We both

agreed on that. But the house—we should really add on. And then there's my job; the case load is humongous."

"You hate it. Quit."

"God, I'd love to. But we can't afford it yet. Henry's right; it was irresponsible. He's furious with me for putting him in this position."

"Putting *him*? He has to be the good guy, doesn't he?"

"He is a good guy." Susan takes a bite and chews thoughtfully, as if she were weighing her proofs. "Did you know he's hiring East L.A. kids as his interns at the agency? We had them over. They love him."

"That's good."

"He wants to do more, get more political in the next two years."

"Like the Benny Wong thing."

"Buddy, yes. And maybe something more visible, like the Save the Reservoir campaign."

"What do you want?"

"It's not that simple." She pokes at her food.

Why not? I want to say. Why can't it be that simple? Isn't that why you marry a dull, nice guy—to keep things simple? I learned it from Dr. Penny: date the interesting ones, but marry the dulls. In college we argued about it on a more literary level—who would we like to spend the rest of our lives with: Mr. Darcy from *Pride and Prejudice*, or *Emma*'s Mr. Knightly? Susan was in the Knightly camp, never wavered.

"It's his character," she'd say.

"Boring evenings around the fire, him poring over the farm accounts, you embroidering a new hankie…"

"Yes," she'd sigh.

"A living death."

"Darcy's a mean bastard."

"Not when you get to know him. I feel we'd get into London more."

"You couldn't depend on him."
"There are other considerations."

After college Susan forgot her own advice for a while. In law school there was a married professor, a doomed liaison that we hashed and rehashed over the long-distance wires. After him, a string of driven fellow-lawyers, then a long dry spell. I'd moved to L.A. by then ("Your room is ready," Susan had written) and I was reading scripts for a producer and specializing in would-be screenwriters with no visible means of support. Patrick was the last of them. He had a job in a bookstore. "Doesn't that make him a little too stable for you?" Susan said. "It's not a real job," I said. "And, anyway, he doesn't have a car."

It was getting close to New Year's, and for once I thought I had it sewn up: the escort, the invitation to a hip party in Silverlake—the ideal "Eve." Susan was feeling particularly, dramatically single and planned to curl up with a Barbara Pym novel and a cup of herb tea until I bullied her into meeting us at the party.

On the way, Patrick and I had a fight over whether he should have changed into a clean T-shirt, and he jumped out of the car at a stoplight. "Yes, I know," I later said to Susan. "Even Darcy wouldn't have done that." She didn't laugh or rub it in. We stood outside in the street and eavesdropped on the conversations floating down to us from the terrace.

"They're talking about decaffeinated coffee," I moaned. "That's not a good omen."

"We can leave now," Susan said. "I'm willing."

"No." I offered her my arm. "We're going in."

It was the night she met Henry. They came that close to missing each other. Fate, swinging forward and back in the minds of two depressed young women on a street in Silverlake. That's how it happens sometimes. And I was fate's handmaiden. If it hadn't been for me their paths might not have crossed at all.

Our entrees arrive.

"So how does it feel?" I ask. "Do you barf a lot?"

"No, I'm feeling great. Ravenous most of the time."

"Eating for two."

"You know, Iz, I might be good at this stuff. Motherhood."

It is said wistfully. She reaches for the Parmesan, and I hack at my calzone through a sudden blur of tears. Why am I crying? I wonder. Why am I the one crying at this table?

I was determined not to weep at their wedding. It was a very conservative show. They picked a Methodist church in Pasadena, generically Protestant, not a curve to be seen in the design of pillar or pew, no blood on its crucifixes. I sat next to an ex-boyfriend of Susan's, one of the lawyers, who dabbed at his eyes through the entire service. When the minister, Dr. Rollins, read from Corinthians, chapter thirteen, the sniffling spread through the congregation.

"Love beareth all things, believeth all things, hopeth all things, endureth all things."

What a shame, I thought, to dangle such fantasies in front of a churchful of keyed-up, suggestible people. Were Susan and Henry putting on this charade for us, or had we demanded it of them? Here we all were, piling our ideals on this couple's shoulders, then sending them off, all by themselves, to find out the ideals were impossible, illusory. Beareth all things, indeed.

Patrick was a no-show that day. All the better, I told myself. Weddings are reputedly a great place to meet men. Susan had insisted I take part in the ceremony in some small way; luckily Henry had a large, dull family that had provided bridesmaids, flower girls, and guestbook attendant. My assignment was to pass out the cake at the outdoor reception. I'd dyed my hair two weeks before, a purplish black, and wore it moussed out and bedecked with a sparkly white bow.

"Doesn't she look like Madonna?" Henry's cousin said.

"Madonna?" Dr. Rollins stared at me in consternation.

"You're Susie's Stanford friend," said Mrs. Henry Sr.

"Yes, that's right." Susan's mother clutched my arm and drew me close so she could whisper, tipsily, "I'm so glad my little girl's not alone anymore." She wiped her eyes with a linen hankie.

"Me too, Mrs. Mullen."

"And you're next, honey. It'll happen for you."

A terrifying thing occurred when they posed for the pictures. As they set up the usual clichés—groom's hand over bride's on the cake knife, etc., one of the cousins shouted: "Get a shot of them feeding each other the cake!" Susan laughingly refused at first; it was one of the traditions she'd sworn she'd never uphold—no garter, no bouquet toss, no cake feeding. But more people took up the cry, like a lynch mob. The photographer handed the couple two small pieces of wedding cake. Henry shrugged and aimed one at Susan's mouth, which was opening up to say "No." Click. Cheers and applause.

I've seen the picture. There's a look of horror in Susan's eyes, made even more sinister by the blurry hand and blob of cake obscuring the lower half of her face. It's the only one of her wedding pictures I can look at and say, "Yes, I know what that person is feeling."

Susan is telling me all about her class-action suit on behalf of two hundred and fifty mental patients in San Diego County. She changed the subject soon after our food arrived. My eyes are dry. We're sipping decaf cappuccinos and sharing a tiramisu.

I murmur agreement at the appropriate moments in her story, ask the right questions, but my thoughts keep returning—foolishly, longingly, to the child I want her to have. It's a picture of Susan, really, from a photograph I saw of her at four, chubby and proud of herself in a new sunsuit, a circular Band-Aid on one knee.

"So I have 'til June to prepare," Susan's saying. "Long enough.

God, I hate going to court." I nod, having lost the drift.

"Susan," I blurt out. "I want you to have the baby."

She blinks a few times, thrown for a minute, groping for words.

"Iz, how sweet. Thanks."

"You're not, though. Going to."

"I can't see it happening that way. There'll be others, right? Plenty of babies."

The old friend in me knows it's time to agree, make her comfortable, but I won't let it go.

"You could just have it and to hell with what Henry says."

She gives me her lawyer face.

"Iz, if you were married I don't think you'd see it that way."

"No, I guess not." She's right, I suppose. What you get from me is the unattached perspective, the solitary point of view. When you catch me promoting parenthood, it's single parenthood I have in mind.

We get up to leave. As we pass, I check out the first-daters' table. They're both digging into gooey desserts. The Inquisitor has fallen silent; a curtain of failure surrounds them. The girl's eyes search the room, pretending to study the paintings. It's too late for deep breaths.

Outside, the night seems colder than it was. Susan and I stroll along Melrose, hands in our pockets, stopping at some of the shop windows to comment on green spandex minidresses and pointy-toed flats. For the first time in ages, I find myself hoping I'll run into Patrick; he lives only a few blocks from here. If I called him from the public phone at the liquor store across the street, would he be cordial, I wonder? Welcoming? Or would he hear it in my voice, would it crack? He never had much tolerance for other people's feelings.

"Here I am." Susan stops at her old Volvo. "Want a ride to your car?"

"It's just around the corner."

"Well, thanks for coming out on such short notice."

"Susan, I feel so bad."

She gives me a hug, a quick one but fierce. It silences me. We say good night.

Driving home to my apartment, I'm building a fantasy in which Susan realizes how much she wants the baby and decides to have it on her own. But really she's not on her own. In one scene, Susan's mother and I are pacing the floor outside the delivery room. (Her mother has stopped drinking completely, she's so moved at the prospect of having a granddaughter.) We pool our resources, rent a small house on a hill in Silverlake.

In a few years the little girl is playing in the yard on a summer night, while we hang out on the porch, drinking coffee and talking every now and then. We're tired—we work hard—but it's a good kind of tired, quiet and complete.

"Bedtime in fifteen minutes," Susan calls to her daughter.

We just sit and watch the sun go down—one of those fat, red suns that seems to linger on the horizon, larger than life.

Mary Ellis

*Here I am, a four-year-old country kid with a strong
maternal streak. I remember stubbornly pushing my dolls in
that buggy back and forth on the dirt road in front of our
house. The wheels would lock up with gravel and I was
forever stopping to clean them off. I laugh looking at this
picture. Some "mother" I was—my purse is plunked right
on top of my "babies."*

Mary Ellis was born and raised in northern Wisconsin and educated at the
University of Minnesota. Her fiction has appeared in the *Wisconsin Academy
Review*, the *Milwaukee Journal's Sunday Magazine*, the *Bellingham Review*, and
most recently in the anthology, *Uncommon Waters: Women Write about Fishing*
(Seal Press).

MARY ELLIS
Wings

If snow falls on the far field,
where travelers
spend the night,
I ask you, cranes,
to warm my child in your wings.

—"Mother's Song," Anonymous
Japanese (ca. 733)

Ever since his brother left for Vietnam, Bill had the same dream. Only it wasn't a dream so much as it was a sensation. It beat across the inside of his eyelids and he could see slits of sunlight as the white feathers expanded to soar on a current of air. He was underneath but he couldn't see anything except the feathers. The wind whistled in his ears and the feathers flapped against the bright yellow sunlight. He was being carried but Bill could not see where and he could not turn his head because it was held in a viselike, even painful grip. Then, when he was listening intently to the melodious whistling, it became shrill and he was suddenly dropped. His arms beat frantically against the wind but they were useless. He heard the sound of his own voice but it did not say what he had intended, what would have been natural. It did not say *Mama!* or *Help!* It said:

"Billy!"

His mother's voice cut through his fall.

"Here," she said, shaking his shoulder. He strained to open his eyes, recognizing that it was still night. He could see the outline of his mother but not the details of her face. She was waving something white in front of him.

"From your brother," she said before dropping it on the covers and disappearing from his room. He pulled an arm out from underneath the covers and groped for the white thing. A letter. Still shaking from his dream, Bill crawled out of bed and onto the floor to the night-light by the closet. He sleepily crossed his legs and ripped the top of the letter open with his thumb. Then he held the seemingly fragile paper under the dim yellow light to read.

Sept-68

Dear Billy Baboon (just kidding),

I know it's been awhile since I wrote to you. We're stuck in the compound this week. It's been hard to get some time alone here. Seems like when that happens, the guys want to play poker or do something. I told them tonight, though, I had to write to my little brother. How are you doing? How's Beans? I just got a letter from Mom so I know she's doing okay. Well, okay enough I guess.

I'm doing okay. Man, you should see the weather here! I'll never complain about another Wisconsin summer again. It gets hotter than hell here, and so muggy that I feel like I'm wet all the time. If you were here, you'd be running around bare-ass naked—except it wouldn't be allowed 'cause you'd be a running target. And not from the VC either. My sergeant says I shoot pretty good. I don't give a damn if I shoot good or not anymore. When I come home, I don't want to see another gun again. Even if I have to bust the ones we have over the old man's head just to get rid of them. And him too.

Did I tell you they call me Elvis Jr? My buddy, Marv, even painted it on my helmet. I don't know why they call me that, all my hair is shaved off. Did you hide all my albums like I told you to? If it looks like the old man is getting close to finding them, take them over to the Morriseaus'. Mrs. Morriseau will keep them for me.

I better go. Keep writing and let me know what's going on there. I'll write again in a bit—hopefully before they send us up to the DMZ—it's still a rumor though. Don't worry, I'll be back soon.

Love James

P.S. I sent Mom some money—don't tell the old man. He'll take it away from her and use it on a beer dream. I sent you some too. Keep it under your mattress, or better yet, hide it in the barn in case of emergencies.

Bill looked down at the two twenty-dollar bills that had slipped out and fallen to the floor while he read the letter. He picked them up and stared at them. He lifted his head, still in the trance of so much money for a nine-year-old boy, and gazed at the twin bed across from him. *James.* Bill's mother always called his brother "Jimmy," but Bill, looking at his brother's empty bed, had always called him "James." Like James Dean, another one of his brother's idols besides Elvis. Or Saint James, although his brother was anything but a saint before he left. There was the good and the bad James, but the letters Bill had gotten so far seemed full of the good James.

Bill crawled back to the bed and hefted the mattress up, slipping the letter underneath to the other letters his brother had sent. This was the first time James had sent money though. He folded the bills in half and tucked them under his pillow. Tomorrow before school, he'd have to think about where in the barn to hide the money and the letters.

He climbed back into bed, pulling the covers up next to his chin. Feeling the coldness of the sheets at the spooky end of the bed, he bent his legs and curled his toes. Since James left, he worried about the safety of his feet so close to where *something* could reach up from underneath the bed and grab them. And no one, not his mother in her frantic few hours of peace, or his father in his Pabst-saturated slumber, would hear him like James.

He turned on his side so he could look again at his brother's bed, covered with a white crocheted spread and untouched now for five months. He thought about the letters lying underneath him, and the ghostly way his mother always brought these letters to him, in his sleep. As though they didn't exist in the daytime. As though his brother didn't exist except at night, a black inky voice on white paper.

The wind whispered through the pine boughs outside his window. He slowly dropped off to sleep again and waited for the feathers.

The next morning, he crept out of the house early, clutching a large blue Mason jar in his arms, and the letters and money stuffed inside his shirt. It was late October and he'd forgotten his jacket in his desperation to get to the barn and back before his parents woke up. By the time he reached the creaky old barn door, he was shaking violently from the freezing morning whip of fall temperatures. He put the money and the letters in the jar and buried it deep in a corner of the barn where he knew the loose hay would be untouched by his father. Peeking out of the barn door at the house to check for signs of life and seeing none, he streaked across the barnyard and slipped back into the house.

"Billy, why don't you want to go outside and play? It's not that cold!" Sister Agnes questioned him at the beginning of the morning recess.

"Nooo," he faltered, and swallowing quickly, came up with an excuse. "I thought I'd practice my penmanship."

The excuse glided across his lips better than he thought, and Sister Agnes beamed with an approving smile.

"All right then."

He watched the long black skirt of her habit glide as smoothly as his excuse out of the door to the playground. He opened his notebook and began to write in his usual scrawly print.

116

Wednesday

Dear Elvis Jr (ha, ha),

*I am doing okay to. I hid the money in the barn. Dad
hasnt found your records. He has been pretti drunk. Mom
and me found him on Saturday in the field sleepng. He
ran over Beans to.*

Bill stopped momentarily and stared out of the classroom
window, the recent death of his dog causing beads of tears to
escape. He wiped them away and continued to write.

*I buryd him behind the barn. Do you use bombs? Will
you teech me how to shoot befor you bust our guns? I am
writng this at school. Its been pretti cold. But no snow. We
are havng turky for thanks givng. Mom says becase your
not here to get a goose. I am going to help Mom bake
cookes. So we can send them to you.*

He heard the wild laughter of many children fill the hallway
outside the door.

Resess is over. I got to go.

Love Bill

He quickly stuffed the letter inside his desk as the room filled
with third-graders.

"How's the penmanship?" Sister Agnes's voice loomed up
behind him.

"Getting better," he answered in a small, tinny voice and tried
to shrink himself further down into his seat.

"That's good," she said, patting his shoulder, her long skirt
brushing past him. He let out a long sigh, relief buoying him
back up to his normal size.

When he got home from school, he'd ask his mother for an

envelope and a stamp, painstakingly writing James's address in small letters so it didn't swamp the front of the envelope the way his writing usually did. Under his address though, in the top left-hand corner, he would write USA in big block letters, and he did the same under James's address with the words SOUTH VIETNAM. Then his mother would take the letter and it mysteriously disappeared until he saw her from the frosted bus windows in the morning thrust two letters (hers included) into the pale gray mailbox that said LUCAS on the side and jack the red flag up.

Every day as the bus rumbled down the gravel road toward town, he'd watch her dwindling figure walk tiredly up the long driveway saluted by red pines until the bus rounded the curve in the road and he could see her no more. She wore the same thing. An old pair of green rubber hunting boots over her slippers, a black-and-white plaid jacket that covered a housedress of faded blue polka dots, and her reddish brown hair still wound in foamy pink rollers that from a distance looked to Bill like newborn mice under the pale blue netting of her nylon scarf. The bus became hushed when he got on, and he fervently prayed every morning that she would wait until the bus rounded the curve before she began talking out loud to the pines as she walked back to the house. That she would keep her hands to her sides until then, before moving them through the cold air as if explaining *something*, as if to touch *someone* strolling beside her.

Then it would start up.

"Hey Luuucasssss," Merton Schmidt would tauntingly croon, sometimes putting a finger up his nose. "Hey Puuccass! How come your mother's crazee and your dad's a stinkin' drunk? Maybe 'cause yr'all LUC-ASSES. Hey! My brother says your brother *should* get a bullet between the ears jus' for bein' a dumb ass and enlistin'! But hey! He's a LUC-ASS, right!" And Merton would laugh so loudly it resonated through the bus like several jackhammers.

Merton Schmidt was thirteen and supernaturally big for his

age. So big that the other kids called him Shithouse Schmidt but never to his face unless they wanted to run for the rest of their tiny lives. Bill's brother even called Merton the "little Hun," but names didn't do Bill any good even though his hatred of Merton outdistanced even Bill's hatred of his father on some days. Bill kept his face pressed to the cold bus window and tried to keep the crying safely down in his stomach or Merton would be on him. He vainly struggled to picture his brother's face, but all he could see was his walking, talking mother in the driveway. He bit his trembling lower lip and gazed out of the window. He ran the same gauntlet of teasing every day.

One morning, after a particularly severe verbal beating from Merton, he turned his face to the window only to see the family's blue Chevy station wagon lodged into the ditch by the curve, and the upper torso of his father hanging out of the driver's window, a smiling haze over his unconscious face. The bus didn't stop.

"Hey Billy!" the bus driver yelled back, "I'll call somebody to haul him outta there when we get to town."

A grin broke across Merton's face and the shots from his mouth began all over again. Bill's nine-year-old heart split open with pain. He stayed huddled in the bus seat, his eyes barely level with the bottom of the window. But he continued to peer out of the window, watching a scattered group of crows circle above the pines and wishing desperately that he were one of them.

Thankfully, Merton rarely rode the bus home from school, catching a ride with his father who worked at the feed store instead. And Bill's mother did not walk down the driveway to greet him when the rattling black-and-orange bus brought him home.

Still, he trusted her more now. Bill ate his grayish brown oatmeal with an island of peanut butter in the middle and watched his mother's eyes drift to the kitchen window from where she leaned against the countertop and stared at the frozen fields and adjoining swamp and woods. He never forgot what he overheard their neighbor, Rosemary Morriseau, say to her husband, although Bill knew it was not meant harshly, just sadly.

"Poor Claire," Rosemary sighed quietly while she washed the supper dishes and her husband, Ernie, polished his boots. Bill pretended to read a book in their living room. "She's three sheets to the wind most days."

He vaguely understood what the expression meant. But what constituted three sheets to the wind? Why not four or five? Or even one? What was a sheet in the wind, Bill pondered with childish bewilderment. A piece of white cloth that got whipped around, if the wind was strong enough that day, and sometimes tangled across the clotheslines. What did that have to do with being crazy?

On the weekends, she wandered through the house during the day, talking and talking, her tired and haunted face appearing in one of the windows every so often when Bill was outside playing. She used to hit him. And shake him until he thought his head would snap off, rolling across the floor like a bowling ball and crashing into the legs of the furniture. That changed after his brother left. When anger flushed her face, she kept her arms and fists locked to herself now, and just yelled at him. Even the yelling had tapered off. She had become, gradually, his ally.

He was being carried again. This time he could look down and the Chippewa River was a black wriggly cord in the landscape seeping beneath him and everything beside it was covered with snow. The whistling filled his head. The grip was not so tight now but it held him firmly. He spread his bare toes and wiggled them in the rushing wind. But it was not cold, it was *warm*, like maple syrup was warm after it settled on his hot pancakes. He spread out his arms to catch the same feeling as his toes. The whistling slowly took on a familiar tune, something he'd heard in the not-too-distant past. He could see his brother's face, his

Brylcreemed hair, and dark, narrowed eyes. What was it? He
listened harder. It was... "My Baby Does the Hanky-Panky"!
"James!" he shouted. It was his brother whistling "My Baby
Does the Hanky-Panky." Bill laughed. He laughed and his heart
felt whole. He laughed at the waves of wind pushing his hair off
his face. And he began to sing...

"Shshsh. Wake up," she said, nudging his head. It was close to
Christmas and another letter floated out of the darkness and onto
his blanket. He blinked, trying to catch the dim outline of his
mother. She caressed his forehead and then was gone. He almost
fell out of bed in his sleepy but hurried effort to get to the night-
light. Then he opened the letter, the whistling still echoing in his
ears.

Nov-68

Hey Bill,

*I can't believe it's going to be Christmas soon. It doesn't
snow here although if you look hard enough at the mountains, you can see a little white—they're mostly purple and
green though. I had a dream the other night that you and
me were down at the river—I don't know—fishing or
something. It was a good dream. I needed it cause it's been
a bad week. Two of my best buddies, Rick and Marv,
walked right into a land mine and were blown up. I wasn't
far behind them. I hit the ground pretty fast and all I can
remember is feeling like my ears were going to split.
Something landed on my back and it turned out to be
Rick's helmet. It also turned out that they didn't walk into
it—Sarg says he saw the wire wiggling, and he yelled but
it was too late. We found the guy dead too, just one
fucking VC by himself. I'm still not feeling so good. I got
some kind of shit growing on my toes too—Sarg says it's
jungle rot—you know—like athlete's foot except it's worse
over here. My feet look like Ma's bread dough. God I
can't wait to come home.*

Say, I'm sorry about Beans. Goddamn the old man.

He's got to fucking destroy everything he touches. He should come over here and trade places with me. I'll bet he'd be one big chicken running through the rice paddies. You know why he's that way? Cause he's SCARED. I used to wonder about him, but since I've been in Nam, I've figured it out. He's fucking scared of everything, but he's really scared of Mom. Cause he knows she's better than he is. When I come home, he better watch out for me cause I'm gonna bust his fucking head.

I'm sorry I couldn't get you a Christmas present. But I sent along some money. I sent Mom some money too and told her to spend it on herself. Make sure she does it, okay? Thanks for the cookies, they were really good. My buddy Hank's sister sent him some cookies, but they were as hard as grenades. After I ate one, I felt like my stomach was gonna blow up too. We used the rest for target practice.

Pray for me. Some days I feel like I'm rotting. Probably cause it's my own damn fault. I guzzle booze over here as much as the old man when I get a chance to. I need to over here, to forget I'm here. Keep writing. The guys think your letters are great. Merry Christmas.

Love you, James

There were splotches in places, where the ink had run slightly. Bill traced a finger across the raised wrinkles in the paper where the splotches were. His brother had been crying. Bill shivered and looked up at the white winter moon framed in his window. Its light reflected off the snow-covered Norway pines next to the house and filled his room with its pale winter glow. He gazed at the moon, absently fingering the money James had sent, seventy-five dollars in all. Bill shivered again. His brother talked to him like he never had before. He talked to him like a *buddy* and not his little brother. He picked up the letter and held it up against the moonlight. It was written in late November, but he didn't know what day or time, and his brother was changing and he couldn't see or touch him.

Bill crawled back over to the bed and lifted the mattress,

stashing the letter and money underneath until morning. Then he grabbed his notebook and pencil from where they lay on the floor at the foot of his bed and crawled back to the night-light. He would cheer his brother up.

Friday

Dear James Dean (ha, ha),

I had a dreem to. Just you and me and we was flying over the river. And you was singng to. And you had wings. But not chiken wings. Big wings. I saw Bunny at the store. She says hi you good lookng devil. Sister says my spellng is gettng beter. I have ben playng with Angel. He is a good dog and Mrs Moriso says I can play with him all I want. But I cant bring him home becase you know. I am going to buy Mom some perfum for Christmas. We sent your presants out last week. Mom cut my hair. Now I dont have none to. My ears get cold. Can I have your red hat? I wont wreck it. I promise. I am writng this in the midle of the night. The moon is realy white. I member the foxs you showd me. Well its like that now. We got lots of snow. Me and Mom are going to church to pray for you. I will be good and pray doubly hard. I got to go to bed now.

Love from your brother,
Billy Baboon

P.S. I will pray for your buddys that got blown up to.

Bill folded the letter and placed it on top of his notebook so he wouldn't forget it in the morning. He climbed into bed, curling himself into a fetal position, and stared at the shadows on the wall made by the snow-laden pine boughs in the moonlight. Christmas was going to be extra hard without James. But he sent money and that would help some. Bill's father, John Lucas, had been drinking more and working less but for the past two weeks he had been gone most of the time, logging for the lumber mill in Olina. He would be back for Christmas, however. Bill pulled the covers up over his face and shut his eyes tightly to bring back the dream. But water squeaked through and he cried himself to sleep instead.

"What does he write when he writes to you?"

Bill looked up from his oatmeal. It was Saturday and he was in no hurry to eat his breakfast. His mother's face was hollow-looking and colorless as though she had not slept. She propped her elbows up on the table and rested her face in her hands.

"What does he write when he writes to you?" she repeated.

"Jus' letters," Bill mumbled. He swallowed another spoonful of oatmeal.

His mother sighed heavily.

"I know something isn't right. But he always says he's fine when he writes to me. And he sends so much *money*."

Bill almost stopped his spoon in midair but caught himself and neatly guided it into his mouth. He felt the blanket of his mother's gaze cover him.

"Billy. Can I read the letters he sends to you? I promise I won't say anything."

Bill quietly placed his spoon on the table. He was hoping she wouldn't ask that. He looked up and silently scrutinized his mother's face. He watched for any sign, a false smile, or too many tears, or even one tear, that might signal her betrayal, signal her old anger that would pull him across the kitchen by his hair if he said no. There was nothing. Nothing but exhaustion so pure it rendered his mother a sagging shell and he thought he could almost see through her to the kitchen sink.

"I'll give 'em to you at lunch. But you gotta give 'em back before..."

But he didn't have to finish because his mother knew. She nodded, reaching out slowly to touch her small son's sand-colored hair. Bill's mouth fell open as he watched her arm extend itself toward him, toward his quivering face, and all he could see and feel was a thin finger of sunlight gently touch his head.

Pray for me.

He always thought of the Sacred Heart Church as a large brick cave. Except that it was dry, not damp, and the cavernous ceiling was covered with frescoes of trumpeting angels and the ascension of the Virgin Mary into Heaven, painted by the German immigrant artists who first settled Olina. It was surprisingly empty even for a Saturday afternoon. He tagged after his mother in the enormous hush of the empty church, trying to keep his bulky winter boots from thumping. There were two votive light stands on either side of the church, placed before the steps to the altar. Four rows of twelve short white candles, most of them unlit, filled the ornate wrought-iron stands. Each stand had a small iron box with a slit in it, for dimes. A dime to light one candle, one lit candle to pray for a beloved's soul, a piece of fire to keep the prayer alive.

As if by silent agreement, Bill and his mother parted ways at the top of the aisle, and she went to the votive stand on the left while Bill knelt at the one on the right. He heard the clink of her dime as she inserted it into the box. She took a long toothpick-sized piece of wood and held it in the flame of an already lit candle until it caught fire. Then she lit her own chosen candle. Bill listened to the low hum of her voice carry through the church as she began to chant the Hail Mary and Our Father. He waited until he was sure she was engrossed in prayer before pulling out a ten-dollar bill from his jeans pocket. He folded the bill into fourths and quickly tucked it through the slit in the box.

He glanced over at his mother. Her head was bent, and her voice, although wavery, didn't stop. He took one of the wooden sticks and held it in the flame of the only lit candle at his stand. He let it burn while the words of Sister Agnes came to him. *These candles are for votive prayers. That means to pray or make a vow, usually for someone else but you can pray for your own soul. The flame of these candles means your prayer burns eternal.*

Eternal meant forever. He lifted his burning toothpick of wood and reached across to the back row of candles. He lit one, two, three... and finally all twelve in that row. Then, snuffing out his stick of wood because it burned too close to his fingers, he reached for and lit another stick. He lit the second row of twelve candles, then the third row, and finally, the fourth row of eleven. He snuffed out his stick and clasped his hands. He squeezed his eyes shut and thought of his brother and his brother's buddies, Rick and Marv. The whistling filled his head. He smiled. "My Baby Does the Hanky-Panky." His face burned and he stopped smiling. He tried to think of a prayer. But the formal prayers of the Church didn't mean anything to him. Then it came to him. He whispered the only thing he could think to say. *Come home, come home, come home, come home...*

"Billy, did you have to light all of them?"

He lifted his head, his face flushed red from heat of the candles, the eternal flame of forty-nine candles blurred in his eyes. *Pray for me*, his brother had said.

"Mom," he answered. "James told me to."

The snowflakes skipped and skidded across the watery blue hood of the car on the way home. The sky was an ancient pearly gray and Bill felt strangely happy. His mother drove, not saying a word, but he could sense that she, too, felt the same as her small son. They had stopped at the drugstore in Olina before driving back out to the farm. She bought him a new shirt and a pair of jeans and a giant solid-chocolate Santa. It was as though she had read his mind when she gave the druggist, Bogey Johnson, a radiant smile and said, "Mr. Johnson, my son would like one of those Santas. Do you think we can oblige him?"

His mother hummed to herself. Bill bit into the fat arm of his Santa and watched the snow-covered field and woods go slowly by as the car crunched over the new snow. Then as the chocolate elbow was melting into the roof of his mouth and they were nearing the farm, his mother braked the car in a series of small jerks and finally stopped it on the shoulder of the road right after they'd cleared the curve. She pulled the packet of letters out of her Wrigley's Doublemint-perfumed purse and laid them on the seat between herself and Bill. The chocolate trickled down the back of his throat.

"Thank you, sweetheart, for letting me read those," she said. She shifted in the car seat so that she faced him. Her face sparkled like the new snow and for the first time that day he noticed that she had taken her pink rollers out. Her reddish brown hair was brushed and sprayed into full curls around her face. She could be, Bill realized, staring dumbfounded at his mother, very pretty.

"You know somethin' " she said matter-of-factly. "Jimmy is gonna come home. I feel it." She placed a clenched hand against her chest and repeated, "I *feel* it.

"You know somethin' else," she said almost gleefully, huddling down in the seat to look Bill in the face.

He shook his head, his eyes fixed on his illuminated mother. He absently bit off the tassel on his Santa's hat.

"*Things*," she emphasized confidently, "are gonna get better.

Hell, they can't get much worse. But you and me and Jimmy can run this farm and make it go. Don't you think so?"

Bill couldn't answer and quietly pushed his bitten-up Santa back into the bag. He cautiously looked back up at his mother. She didn't seem to notice his lack of response and had shifted forward in the car seat again. But her face was no longer jubilant, it was sad and tears ran down her face.

"You know I love you boys... very much. But," she said softly, looking through the windshield at their house in the distance nestled among the red pines, "if I'd have had wings, I would've been gone a long time ago."

Dec-68

Dear Bill,

I know this letter is coming pretty fast right after the last one but Sarg said there would be a special pick-up for holiday mail. It's raining and I'm writing this inside a tank. Remember how much I used to love the sound of rain on the roof? Except Beans always howled like he was dying or something when it rained. I'm sorry that I threw my boot at him that time and hit him in the head. Then he really started howling, remember? Anyway, it rains like it's going to flood here. Listening to it makes me kind of sleepy. I pretend sometimes, when we can't hear any shooting or bombing, or even when the jets (we call them warbirds) are gone for a little while, that I'm home. Or when that doesn't work, I pretend this is a real country. It is a real country but sometimes I feel like I'm floating just above the ground and I can't touch it. And other times, I feel like I'm in a doll house—cause American soldiers are so big, me included. The Vietnamese are the size of you, Bill. I'm a giant compared to them. I guess you could have joined the army with me after all (ha, ha).

We were cutting trail through some jungle near the DMZ two days ago, and I barely missed stepping into a pungee pit. The VC dig these holes, and then put bamboo spikes in the bottom. They cover the holes up with leaves and even buffalo shit so you can't see them. If you step in one, the spikes go right up through the bottom of your boots and up into your legs. It scared the shit out of me.

Don't tell Mom, but I caught some shrapnel in my arm. The medic just cleaned it up and gave me a shot of penicillin. It's not that bad. Is Mom okay? Her last letter was strange.

Thanks for your letter—it was great! And it got here pretty fast too. You can wear my hat and I don't care if you wreck it. I'm not going to wear it again anyway. Hey! I'm glad I don't have chicken wings—they'd never get me off the ground.

The other day I saw a really big bird flying over. Like a heron, only bigger. I asked one of the ARVNs what it was. (ARVN stands for Army of the Republic of Vietnam—one of the Vietnamese fighting on our side.) He said it was a crane and laughed at me. He said didn't you ever see a crane before? I guess we have them in Northern Wisconsin, but they usually stay in Southern Wisconsin. They're beautiful, Bill. I hope I see more of them. But they must get hit in the cross-fire and bombing. I wish I could have wings like a crane. Seeing that crane reminded me of the geese in the fall. I really missed seeing the geese this year.

Here's a picture of me. I look pretty dirty, but that's the way it is when we're out here. Thanks for the presents and the fruitcake. Well, little man, I've got to go. Give Mom a hug for me. Tell the old man to piss-off (just kidding— don't do it). Say hi to the Morriseaus if you see them.

Love James

Bill stared at the Polaroid of his brother under the night-light. He had his helmet on so Bill couldn't see how short his hair was, but the rest looked reasonably enough like James. Except his smile wasn't real. His mouth looked as though invisible fingers had taken his lips prisoner and pulled them sideways, the skin unnaturally tight underneath his nose. His eyes were sunken and dark, and it was clear that his brother had lost some weight. Besides the picture there was more money still, and Bill counted five ten-dollar bills. He leaned back against the wall. *Little man.* That's how he felt, as though when his brother left all the unspoken reasons for James's leaving suddenly descended upon Bill, and in his awareness of them, he became old.

It was a week past Christmas. Bill's father had come home, drank and slept through Christmas Eve and most of Christmas Day, getting up only to eat the holiday meal. It surprised Bill, covertly watching his father eat his turkey, how little he knew or cared about the tall, pasty-skinned man at the head of the table. His nine-year-old life had revolved so intensely lately around his daily struggle to survive at school, the strained wait for his brother's letters, the fields, the woods, the swamp, and the sky of their farm, and lastly, the fragile web of his mother's world, that he had forgotten to be cautious around the beer-reeking presence that he'd been avoiding, it seemed, since he was born. He silently ate a forkful of stuffing before catching his mother's eye. A small conspiratorial smile passed across her lips. Her dark eyes had lost their dull captive look and shined. *Things are gonna get better.* He glanced down again to the far end of the table where his father sat, and felt an unfamiliar stab of pity. James was thousands of miles away from them in a country that even Bill, in his enormous capacity for imagination could not imagine but only carried with him in the word *Vietnam.* A country of purple mountains, man-made woodchuck holes that stabbed, wriggling barbed-wire bombs, a bird that flew bigger than a Canada goose, and hot metal that flew like a bird. Yet, Bill knew it was his father, not his brother, who was in a strange country he'd never get out of; a country where only he thought as he did, and whose borders he broke through occasionally to hit his wife, to despise his sons.

Still now that John Lucas was home for the holidays, Bill wondered how he was going to survive without his brother there to shield him, to shield her. But in his small head he knew, survive he must. James would come home. And James would tell the priest that what he preached at the Christmas mass was wrong. The loving brotherhood of man did not exist.

Sunday

Dear James,

Mom and me prayd for you. I ate alot of choclate at Christmas and got sick. Dad got firrd and is home now. Me and Mom went sledding. She lost some of her curlers but did not get mad. She sat in front so I wouldnt get hit by snow. I am back at school. Sister says to look for Janury stars. Do you have stars over there? We saw a big white owl sittng on the fence by the barn. Mom says it is a snowi owl from canada. She says he came to visit us becase he ran out of food in canada. Mom cryd. She says you shoulda went to canada to. I said, mom, if they dont got any food, why should James go there.

Bill stopped. He could hear his mother shouting in the kitchen and the banging of pots and pans. His father's deep rumbling voice answered her. Bill tensed up. Then he heard a heavy thump. His mother shouted some more. Bill sighed.

Can they let you out earli?

Bill raised his pencil from the paper. Now he could hear his mother sobbing.

Please come home. I am scard. I like your picture. Can I have your helmit when you come home? Mr. Moriso says he will take me and you to show us the crans. He says they fly by lake superier. They say hi. If they let you out earli will you come home? I got to go to bed now.

Love Bill

He put his notebook down. His mother's crying was ebbing. Bill crawled back into bed and covered his ears against the muted notes of her sorrow. It was the middle of January, the middle of a freak midwinter thaw. The chickadees had broken into their spring song that day. Bill had opened his window to the unseasonably warm wind and it blew the ivory curtains into midnight dancers. He felt both elated and ashamed, having betrayed his fear to his brother. But as much as he wanted to destroy what he had written, he also felt sure that it would bring his brother home. Maybe, he thought, listening to the melting ice drip from the eaves, he could even persuade his mother to call the Army and tell them that James was needed at home. That he had made a mistake by enlisting.

Bill turned to lie on his right side. He tried not to think of tomorrow. Tomorrow was school. Tomorrow meant Merton. He stared at the dancing curtains. Their fluttering hypnotized his already tired eyes and, combined with the soothing plunk, plunk of the melting ice, his eyes closed. Tomorrow was not now.

The wings flapped, enclosing Bill for a few seconds and brushing his face and chest. They opened again, lifting upward against the surging wind, and he raised his eyes to see that the white wings spanned an enormous length from side to side. His bare legs swung back and forth and he was held this time by his shoulders. The air was heavy and moist. So moist that he felt slippery like a fish and as helpless as one, clutched in the talons of an eagle. But his shoulders felt no pain, just roped and secure. He dropped his head against his chest and looked below.

They were passing over the Morriseau farm with its two silos and big duck pond. The eighty-acre field behind their house was filled with little clouds of dust, each one exploding like spores from the head of a smashed puffball mushroom. Poof! Poof! Poof! they went. Little black specks were chaotically running through the field and every time a speck hit one of the clouds, it burst into flames, becoming a ball of fire. He could hear shouting and the deep pop and zing of rifles going off. The air became thick and choking with dust. Bill's small chest caved in and his lips quivered. He coughed hard and his hands jerked up toward his mouth.

Then the wings came together again, enclosing his small body in a cocoon of feathers. When they opened, he saw that the field was clear and a cloud of cowbirds dipped and circled beneath them. His chest cleared and he no longer felt like crying. He heard the high, clear notes of whistling and looked down. There was someone standing in the middle of the grassy field, waving and waving. The wings caught an upcurrent of air and they glided toward the far end of the field. They cruised its wide square edge before coming back around.

Bill cried out. It was James, wearing a dull green helmet that had **Elvis** painted in black letters on the side, and balancing a rifle across his shoulders. He dropped the rifle and waved with both hands.

"Hey Billy! Hey Billy Baboon! It's me! It's your brother!"

"Jaaaamess! Jaaamess!" Bill shouted but the wind took his voice and it disappeared in the rush of air between the feathers above him.

"Over there!" his brother shouted, and picking up his rifle, pointed with it toward their own field. A single black speck was running over the brown plowed earth. The wings caught the cue and flapped harder. They closed the distance in a few seconds and swept lower. Bill screamed joyfully.

"Shithouse! You better run! You're up shit creek now!"

Merton was desperately running and tripping over the deep furrows in the field. Bill pulled his legs up to his chest and curled his toes. They dropped altitude and cruised right up behind Merton. Bill lowered his legs and hooked his feet under Merton's arms. With legs suddenly as strong as steel cable, he lifted the squirming tonnage of a boy into the air twenty feet before dropping him.

"Don't hurt the little Hun! Jus' scare 'im!" he heard his brother shout.

Merton hit the soft plowed earth with a thump and a groan. But he got up and began running again, his head swiveling to pinpoint Bill's location. Bill whooped. Merton, his eyes rolling wildly, ran harder. Again, they came off a large current of air to level themselves behind the nemesis of Bill's days. This time Bill did not pick him up, but, with legs wound tight as springs against his chest, aimed and kicked, knocking Merton between the shoulder blades. Merton went down so hard he bit into the overturned field and ate dirt. He stayed down, breathing hard, grinding and spitting dirt. But he was not hurt, just scared. Bill stared at the sprawled-out boy as the wings lifted him back into the sky. Then as quickly as the desire for revenge had come, it had also gone, and they left the Lucas field with its cleaved and unplanted earth and returned to his brother standing almost perfectly camouflaged with his green jungle uniform in the middle of their neighbor's lush grassy field.

James had taken off his helmet and stood smiling broadly up at Bill. The wings, despite their massive size, lowered Bill until the bottoms of his feet touched his brother's shaved and bristly head. Bill could not speak. *This is not a dream. That's really my brother.* The wings didn't lower him any farther and they hovered while Bill's feet curled around and hugged his brother's head. A look of pain crossed his brother's face. James reached up and encircled Bill's ankles with his hands, kissing the bottoms of his little brother's feet.

"Man! It's really good to see you, Billy Baboon," his brother said softly. "Really good."

James released one of Bill's ankles and swept his arm in a semicircle around him.

"I dream about this place all the time...yeah, all the time. I told Ma I never wanted to see this place again and that I wasn't comin' back. I told her..." his brother stopped in a half-sob, half-yell, gripping Bill's ankle so tight it hurt, "that she didn't know a fucking thing! But she did know. She *does* know."

He kissed Bill's foot again.

"Don't ever leave here, Bill. You and me... we'll have some fun when I come home."

The wings flapped. Bill strained, stretching his legs as far as he could to touch his brother's head. But the wings lifted him higher and higher. His brother put his helmet back on and picked up his rifle. He wiped his face on his sleeve and stared up past Bill to the wings. James opened his mouth as if to say something but shut it again, raising his hand slightly while a deeply troubled look passed over his face.

"I gotta go. But don't worry. I love you, Billy! And Elvis," James said, pointing to his helmet, "loves you too!"

Bill watched James run from the field and disappear into the swamp on the edge. His heart beat against the wall of his chest. He heard the high notes of whistling echo from the swamp, and smiled through his tears. "My Baby Does the Hanky-Panky." He tried to cry out. Nothing. He listened to the lingering sound of whistling and then it struck him. If his brother had been down there, who was above him, carrying him?

He stretched his neck to look up, but all he saw was sunlight, bright yellow and blinding. The wings flapped, covering his face, tickling and brushing his cheeks. A high guttural call pierced the air around him. The wings swept forward and covered him for the last time, enveloping him with the more familiar feel of his sheets and blankets, and with the descending silence of dreamless sleep.

Stephen Dixon

STEPHEN DIXON
Novelist and short story writer

∫*nterview*

by Linda Davies

When we initially asked Stephen Dixon to do an interview with us, he was, shall we say, reluctant: "Believe me, you'd be disappointed in anything I said and would wonder why you asked and then you'd have to make some strong moral decision as to whether you should go ahead with it because you asked for it. I'll save you the trouble and qualms. I have nothing to say and every time I say something, it only confirms it. The only thing I'm good for is writing, and that's debatable. I only want to write;

Stephen Dixon

I don't want to speak. Frog's interview [from his novel **FROG***] says most of it for me. The interviewer's judgment at the end would be yours too, but perhaps you, knowing me longer, would be more sympathetic and understanding."*

So, we asked if perhaps a written interview would be more palatable.

DAVIES: *It is my guess that writing is more than something you choose to do, that it is something you must do. What is the feeling like that drives you to your typewriter or word processor or whatever?*

DIXON: Writing's something I chose to do after I felt I failed at every other kind of artistic expression. I was a lousy actor, but I wanted to be an actor. I did nothing original in acting and could barely take the anxiety of appearing on stage in front of audiences, and also found it very tedious to learn lines. I tried painting, but I'd knock off a painting in a few hours and then what would I do? Later on, after I'd been writing for twenty years, I took up painting and drawing again and got very much involved in it and became a painter-writer, alternating, which was exciting, for I was expressing myself in two ways in one day, but that only lasted a few years and then writing became harder and I felt I had to devote myself to the thing I thought I did best and got the most satisfaction out of, and that was writing but only by a few inches.

I wrote poetry too, but wasn't a good poet and didn't take the time to become one. I also couldn't stand forms. I never knew what a sestina was; I tried to learn but always forgot. One doesn't need to know things like that to be a poet, but poetry seemed a more formal form of writing than I wanted, and it also didn't take as much time as I wanted writing to do. But the feeling that drives me to my typewriter—and it *is* a typewriter, a manual, and it's always been a manual—once I'm working on a story, it's easy to answer what the feeling's like. It's to complete the story. But once a story's completed, the feeling's different. It's to start a new one, or to continue a novel. I am a driven writer; I don't feel good when I don't have something to write. So I write every day and after I finish a story or novel, I start another story or novel the next day. The feeling that drives me is a sweaty, anxiety-ridden feeling; it insists I start something, try something, try many things, till I have something to write the next day. Writing is a wonderful torment; it's banging your fists against the wall till you have something you've written. I'm an angry person and writing releases that anger daily.

If your life circumstances prevented you from writing, how might this drive manifest itself?

What would I do if I didn't write, was unable to, in other words? Well, that's too hypothetical a question. What would prevent me? An accident to my hands so I couldn't type? Then I'd memorize stories, line by line, work over them in my head daily, till I was able to write them orally into a cassette player. No, I missed the question. Maybe because it seems impossible that any life circumstances might prevent me from writing. The worse the circumstances, the more I'm motivated to write. I don't look for horrible circumstances, but I've lived through many horrible circumstances by writing. I've come through them, in other words. There isn't a horrible circumstance I couldn't write about, for through writing about it I'd come to understand that circumstance more clearly. Writing's finding yourself, that's what I've found. I learn about things, myself, other things, things I go through, things other people go through, through writing. There could be other ways, but to me this is the best way. Better than painting, better than acting. Many times I discover not only what I know but, more importantly, what I'm feeling through my writing.

You seem extremely modest in your opinion of your own work; certainly you are not cocky, as one could easily be, having written so much widely read and appreciated work. What do you suppose people find so appealing?

Modesty? Why not be modest? Try being cocky in what you're doing and you lose it. You think you've done it so don't need to do it, perhaps. I haven't got time for being anything but modest. Meaning: finish one thing, on to the next thing. I like what I'm doing at the time I'm doing it, but that's as far as my feeling toward my work goes. Once it's done, it's done. I don't look back and think I did something good there; nah, I go on and on and on, for I'm much too obsessed a writer to look back and take gratification in what I've done. I want to forget what I've done and write as if I've never done anything. It keeps things surprising; it makes the writing exciting—but all this might be too immodest a thing to say about what I do. And I don't know if I'm widely read. I don't get much feedback and I'm glad I don't. I write, I send out, I accept the rejections as gratifyingly as I accept the acceptances; in time, everything seems to get placed. What is there to be cocky about? The number of stories written and published, the number of books published? They are nothing to me. What is [important] to me is what I'm doing now, and if I've finished something now, what I'm doing next. For I always want to do something new, and what I've done is old. The second I finish it, it's old, it's done, it's gone, and it's on to the next.

And what do I suppose people find so appealing? It's tough to say. I don't want to say. Maybe the humor, maybe the drama, maybe the things I dig deep into, maybe the clarity, and maybe the denseness, and maybe the tricks, and maybe what might seem new. I don't know; I'm stumped here. I don't write to be appealing and I doubt I am to many readers. I don't know what works in my writing, and I don't care. If I like it, that's all that matters to me. It might be a terrible thing to say—it sounds so, well, self-centered, self-directed—but it's for me only I write, and then I send it out because just maybe someone else might like it too, for whatever reason. I didn't make much sense there because it's too difficult a question to answer; because it deals with a part of myself I don't want to face, the mysterious part that perhaps writes the stories and the only part of myself I don't want to go into in a self-exam like this, or in my writing. It seems a restricted area.

I've heard some people feel a certain part of their head is producing a story. Someone I know feels it slightly above and behind their eyes. Do you feel activity in a particular part of your head when you write?

What part of the head? I can't place what part. I've said before that writing a first draft of a story—and this is the most important draft for it's essentially the genetic makeup of the story—is like having a hole pop out of my forehead and the story spilling forth like champagne froth. The story keeps bubbling out like that till the first draft's done. Most times there's no chance I can recork the bottle. In other words, it's whole-headed activity, and once the head's emptied of the story, the first draft is done. How I uncork that bottle is another thing. I sit down in front of my typewriter; it's the day after I've finished a short story and have sent it out. And then I start typing. First words that come— ninety percent of the time—are usually the first words of the story, though with some refinement in the rewriting later on. I might have to write three first drafts of a story, or three different stories in first draft, but all in one day till I feel I finally have the first draft I want to work on or have a story to work on. The first draft can take me an hour or two but the rewriting, which starts the next day, can go on for a month or months.

Your hands. We find we want to ask you these odd questions. I think it's because your stories seem to come so much from your head in some ways, yet, for instance, your reference to your relationship with your children—or to your fictional children in your stories—is so down to earth, so attentive, that we imagine your hands to be very solid, practical parts of you. Is that so?

My hands probably got solid through thirty-five years of constant manual typing. I've done a good amount of heavy labor with those hands, too. My hands need activity and they need a manual to bang a story out on. I love manuals because they provide me with keyboard action, the same kind a pianist has. No tinkling for me; I bang, crash, hit, stick my keys and punch holes into my roller and make mincemeat of my ribbons. I am an aggressive writer and a forceful typist; writing's a very physical activity for me. As for my relationship with my children, I can't tell you here what they mean to me. It's a very strong feeling I have for them, and strong feelings are what I write about almost exclusively. Writing's emotion above everything else.

Do you keep a "to-do" list? If so, what's at the top of your list?

No to-do lists since I wouldn't be able to find them. Besides, I keep whatever I want to write in my head. In addition, I know what should be at the top of a to-do list; it's always the same: take care of my family, write, work, keep going, try to stay healthy so you can do the other things. There isn't much else that means anything. I read a lot, but that's not a must-do or to-do, it's simply a do-do.

Please tell us the first story or book that you remember ever reading.

First stories or books I read were fairy-tale books with beautiful, colorful Victorian illustrations. They were around the house when I was growing up and I read them. I think the first book I ever read in its entirety was *Toby Tyler Goes to the Circus.* I liked his name and I wanted to run away to the circus too. I think the second book I read in its entirety, but without understanding what I was reading, was Turgenev's *Fathers and Sons.* I thought it was a children's book, since it had illustrations, and the title also made it seem that way.

It seems likely that your style must have driven your early school-teachers crazy. When did you finally feel that someone got what you were trying to do?

My style didn't drive anyone crazy at first because I didn't have a style till my thirties. My early style was readable and functional and forgettable and inimitable because nobody would want to imitate it since it was the style of other writers, Hemingway and Saroyan, mostly. As to someone finally getting what I was trying to do? It wasn't so much that as it was hearing my older brother Jim laughing in the next room in Washington, D.C., when he came down for a visit and I was working there. I'd given him a story of mine to read, one of the first I'd written. I was twenty-three, and he was a fiction writer, and I felt if I could get him to laugh at my story—though I didn't try to get him to laugh; he just laughed—then perhaps I was doing something all right with my budding fiction, since he was a guy whose opinions and reactions I respected. That's all. I didn't need much. One brother laughing at one of my early works kept me writing for a few more years.

What kind of music do you like?

Classic, serious, everything from Gregorian chants to what I consider the good serious-modern: Bartok, Stravinsky, Messiaen, John Adams, Arvo Pärt. I dislike sentimental, romantic, vulgar, loud, obtuse, shallow, stupid, childish, commercial music. As in all the art I like, it's got to be serious, meaning: probing exploring, deep, human-shaking, for its time making new ground, and it has to move me. I admire clever art but I only love art that moves.

What are your first and second memories of your life?

Hard to tell. My memory does me in most times, and I think one of the reasons I write is to recall. I do have one ancient memory of being smaller (standing up) than an average bed and trying without success to climb onto it. Also: late evening car rides home with my family and my father lifting me out of the back seat and carrying me to bed, putting me under the covers, tucking me in, my mother later coming into the room and kissing my forehead good night.

I feel a sense of panic in some of your work. Do you feel that when you write?

Panic in my work? I don't feel panic when I write, but I do feel very strong emotions. I'm worried about a lot of things, mostly my children and wife now, and I've had a few brushes with things that have caused a certain anxiety about life which has perhaps entered into my fiction.

If your name weren't Stephen Dixon, what would it be?

If I weren't Stephen Dixon, I'd be Stephen Ditchik, the name I had before my parents changed it when I was five, in kindergarten, having just learned through painstaking practice how to write my last name. Then I had another name to learn to write and "Ditchik" I could forget. But I wouldn't want to be anyone else but who I am. That doesn't mean I'm satisfied with who I am; just means I wouldn't want to chance another life. None of it is easy, almost all of it is difficult, and sandwiched in between are some good moments everyone has.

Stephen Dixon

*This was taken in New York City on Broadway in the
80's on one of the few afternoons after school and on
weekends when I wasn't working at a job, which could
account for the smile: I was with my friends, it was warm
out, and I was free.*

Stephen Dixon has published fourteen books of fiction: nine story collections
and five novels, including *FROG*—an interrelated collection of novels,
novellas, and stories—which was a finalist for the 1992 PEN/Faulkner Fiction
Award as well as being a finalist for the 1991 National Book Award. Dixon has
published about 350 stories in various magazines since 1963, when his first,
"The Chess House," was published in *Paris Review*. The two stories he's had
published in *Glimmer Train Stories,* "The Stranded Man" and "Many Janes,"
will be in a collection published at the end of the year by British American
Publishing, called *Moon*.

Dixon teaches in the Writing Seminars at Johns Hopkins University.

STEPHEN DIXON
Many Janes

ive me a line. One night when I was sleeping a dream appeared to me. Wrong. A line. I woke up, got my socks on, shorts, put on my watch, strode down the hall, went to the toilet, had breakfast, dressed, or dressed and had breakfast, read a book first, made love to my wife, it's night, before I woke, I'm in bed, wife comes to bed, wife's about to come to bed, "Come to bed, wife," she does, love, sleep, wake up, toilet, dressed, breakfast, work. Forgot my watch. I call home and she says "It's right here where you left it," and I say "Where?" and she says "On the night table by your side of the bed where you always leave it when you go to sleep," and I say, I say what? I don't say "Ship it," since I'm only ten minutes away by car, I say "Please, I have tremendous difficulty without my watch, so imagine it on my wrist and I bet it'll be there," and she says "That's ridiculous," and I say "Hold it in your palm, close your eyes and imagine it on my left wrist, please," and she says "All right, little to lose," and next thing I know, thirty seconds at least, it's not on my wrist. I jump out of bed, toilet, dress, don't forget to shave, shave, downstairs, wake the kids, wake them, prepare their breakfast, no wife, just me and the kids, no woman, from downstairs "Kids, come on, I don't hear any rustling, get up, school, breakfast, I mean breakfast and then school, don't forget to wash your face and brush your teeth and hair, in whatever order you wish but the brushing with the two different kinds of brushes," still don't hear anything, "Kids, please, I don't want you to be late again, it's embarrassing to me and also makes me late for work," no reply or movement, I call their names, listen, go upstairs, door's open because I opened it when I woke them before, they're sleeping or pretending to or one's doing one and other the other, I let up the shade, should have done that when I first woke them, kiss their foreheads which I did before, muss their hair, rub their shoulders, except for the kissing I can do each of these at the same time since there's little space between their beds, room's very small and really only for one person but since their mother died two years ago they want to sleep in the same room, they stir, I say "School, up, face, teeth, hair, breakfast, long-sleeved shirts today, feels a bit chilly out," and my oldest, whose bed I'm sitting on now, says "I don't want to go to school," and I say "Heard that one before," and youngest says "I don't want to either," and I say "Come on, don't make me raise my you-know-what," and the youngest says "What?" and I say "Long-sleeved shirts, bit chilly out," look in four of the five dresser drawers, two for pants, two for shirts, top mutual one's for their underclothes, pajamas, tights and socks, find two matching shirts and pants, put them on their beds, "Fresh socks and underclothes today, now up and out, you've five minutes to do everything I said to and get downstairs, starting now," and I look at my watch, or rather my wrist for my watch isn't on it, go into my room and look where I always put it when I go to sleep, night table on the right side of the bed, side Jane slept on and where I mostly sleep now, not there, yell out "Either of you kids see my watch?" no answer, go into their room, "Anyone see my watch?" blank stares, they're dressing now, look sleepy, both have their momma's long thick thighs and full tushy. "Don't forget to brush your teeth." "Brushed it when I went to sleep," oldest says, and youngest "I did too." "Bad breath in the morning, even I smell it, so you want to make your mouth fresh. Do it for me, for yourselves, for your teachers and friends. But my watch, I can't leave here without it." "Maybe you left it downstairs by the record player, I see it there a lot," oldest says. I go downstairs, it's there, I put it in my wallet, my pocket, what did I mean "my wallet" and why not just put it on my wrist?— no time—put water on for coffee, bring their food to the table, make and pack their lunch, mix juice up and fill their thermoses and stick all this into their schoolbags. It'd be nice if I had a wife and she was pregnant—always wanted three—but not so pregnant where she couldn't help me get the kids off to school, just someone else around here, much as I love them, and for of course other reasons, phone rings, who can it be so early? I think. It's my second wife, at the airport, decided to take the red-eye special rather than leave this morning, "If there's not too much traffic I should be home in an hour." "I'll wait for you but in the meantime take the kids to school." "Jane will be here in an hour," I say to them. "Good," both say, and youngest "She have her baby yet?" "If she had don't you think you would have heard about it? No, let me rephrase that and also apologize to you, since it wasn't nicely said. You would have known if she had the baby, sweetheart, since you two will be the first to know after me." "And the doctors and nurses of course," and I say "Of course," and take them to school, come home, Jane's there, we make love, Jane's there, we kiss, she's having coffee, Jane's there, I say "Hi, hello, you look exhausted, I missed you, I'm so horny for you, let's go upstairs or do it right here on the chair," "I'm ready," she says, Jane's there, she says when I say some of that "I'm feeling a little nauseous, maybe from all the traveling, so possibly tonight?" Jane's there, a photograph of her, on my night table, dead now five years, one of her nursing the youngest with the oldest standing beside her chair holding her hand, she was in the car of a friend when it ran off the road and hit a rock, on a train that hit a train and several people in her car died, flying home from an academic convention I'd told her it was futile going to since with the new baby and the one we wanted to have a year from now she wouldn't be able to work for a couple of years, drowned while swimming, I swam out but couldn't reach her in time, in a boat that capsized, kids had life jackets on but were struggling in the water hysterically and seemed to be drowning, "Save the girls," she said, "I'll try to swim to shore," "You can do it?" because she was seven months pregnant, eight, weeks from delivery, "You really think it smart for me to get in this boat?" she'd said, "Just save the girls, I'll make it," I grabbed the girls, one in each arm, and started swimming to shore on my back, "Jane, are you near, are you swimming?" I yelled as I swam, "The girls, I'll be okay," got them to shore, looked quickly at the lake and saw little waves but not Jane, made sure the girls were breathing, said "Stay here, I'm going for Mom," looked for her, screamed her name, no one was around, no houses, cars, plane overhead, "Jane, Jane," jumped in the water and swam to where I think I last saw her, "Yes, dear, what is it? You must be having a bad dream," we're in bed, kids in the next room in theirs, "Should I turn on the light?" "Turn it on," I say, she does, "I'm all right now, don't worry, turn it off, the light's blinding," she does, I feel for her body in bed, it's not there, of course it's not, she died a year ago, longer, I hear my youngest daughter snoring in the next room, something to do with the adenoids, year ago doctor said she should have them removed, then Jane got very sick very quickly, weeks after she was diagnosed she dies, baby she was carrying with her, nothing's been done about the girls' health except their semiannual teeth and annual eye examinations, both wear glasses, I wear them, Jane wore them, the baby in a few years probably would have worn them, it's morning, I wake up alone, it's an apartment, no kids, I go to the bathroom and wash up, do a few exercises, in front of the bathroom mirror and on the bedroom floor, shower, shave, brush my hair, I should get a haircut I think, I'll get one during lunch, put my watch on, dress, put my wallet and keys in my pants pockets, tie on but don't tie it tight at the neck, kitchen, breakfast, get the newspaper from in front of the front door first and read it while drinking coffee and eating toast, news is awful today, or maybe I'm not in the right mood for hard news,

turn to the arts section, book by a beautiful young woman, or at least her photo makes her beautiful, hand sweeping back or holding in place her long dark hair, I fantasize getting up with her in the morning, her name's Jane, previous night our first time in bed, review's a good one, "witty, warm and wise," which is what they seem to say about most of these first novels by young women, I take the subway to work, she's on the subway reading the paper with one hand and other hand clutching the pole, I think should or shouldn't I?—absolutely don't pass the chance up, I push through some people between us and say "This is amazing—I mean, excuse me, Miss, but you are Jane so and so— I either forgot or didn't catch your last name so no offense meant with that 'so and so'—the writer, in this same paper, the book review today?" and she says "That's right," "Well, congratulations, a terrific review," and she says "Thank you, and my stop's coming up," making a move for the door as the train pulls into the station," and I say "Mine too, and that's the truth—a coincidence rather than a ruse," and she says "I believe you, why wouldn't I?" and we get off and I say as we leave the station "Do you have to work too because the writing doesn't pay sufficiently, or maybe you have an early appointment with an agent or editor, or is that too personal a question and assumption, which if it is I'm sorry," and she says "No, it's not, and yes, I work," "Where, at what?" and she tells, we're on the street now and she says "Well, it's been nice talking but I'm a little late," and I say "You going this way?—me too, and again, coincidence, no ruse, Galaxy Imports, Hundred-eight Water," and after several seconds of silence while we walk—I've looked her over, she's sweet-looking rather than beautiful, nice shape and gait too— and when I don't know if I should say this, but what the hell, do, for lots to gain but not much to lose, "You have children, married, leave someone at home, or is it just you, or are all those again too personal as questions and assumptions?" and she says "Just me," and I say "Just me too," and then "How long'd it take to write the book?—I've always been curious about that and the intricacies of it, and this time I won't wait till a book comes to the library or out in paperback before I get it, something I probably would never do despite the good review unless I had met you, I don't know why, money perhaps, laziness I presume," and she says "Maybe fiction isn't one of your main interests," and I say "But it is, reviews of them the first thing I turn to in the paper if the front-page news isn't an event," tell her what I'm presently reading and have recently read, she tells me what she thinks of these books, more questions, answers, and assumptions from both of us till we're in front of my office building and I say "Maybe you won't want to, I'm sure short time we've spoken you don't see much reason why you should, but would you like to meet for lunch today?—I was going to get a haircut but I can do that after work," "Sure, where?" We meet, have dinner the next day, make love the following week, I move into her apartment and sublet mine, hers is much nicer and she preferred it that way, marry, two girls, she dies, I meet and marry another woman named Jane, I don't look for them with that name, just the only kind I seem to find, she dies, another woman named Jane, Jane Jane Jane, my three Janes, I have four daughters altogether with them, the fourth is named Janine but after her mother dies I call her Jane, they grow up, move out, I retire from work, buy the cabin we always rented summers for a month and winterize it and move in there, the town's librarian's named Jane, I say "That's a coincidence, and this is no ruse, really, and of course it's one of the more common names, but my three wives were all named Jane," and tell her they all died of natural causes only and that I loved dearly each one, she's much younger than I, I'm attracted to her and now maybe even her name and like the selection of new books the library gets and go to it almost every day it's open, she invites me to her house for dinner, I invite her out to a movie, we hike up the one monadnock in the area and picnic there, make love, marry, I don't want another

child but she does for she never had one so we try, it's a girl, I
wake up, put my watch on, take it off, exercise, jog in the park
a couple of miles, shower, coffee, dress, leave for school, leave
for the office, leave for work, subway, bus or car, when I get
there I see my watch is gone, must have come unclasped and
slipped off without my knowing it, I buy a new one at lunchtime
when I'd planned to get a haircut, same cheap kind, runs on time,
come home from work, make several calls, none of the women
I speak to seems interested in going out or staying in or really
doing anything with me and this time each of them, perhaps
because I'm so eager to see someone I persist in trying to
persuade them, says it, wonder how I'm going to meet one for
I'm getting close to middle age and might even be in it, since I'm
not sure when it starts, and want to marry and have children or
a child, maybe if I took an evening course at a continuing-ed
school, one that lots of relatively young women attend or at least
hang around the school's bookshop or cafeteria, or one during
my lunch hour: writing, painting—maybe the model, a painter
or writer earning a few extra bucks, she's wearing only a
bathrobe, walks around the room during her break looking at
the students' work of her, says something to me about mine, "I
have breasts as big and fat as that?—boy, are you fantasizing," or
"It's quite good," or "I'd go easy on the shadowing and multi-
layers of paint if I were you, but I should mind my own
business," and I say "Thanks," or "No, thanks, do you paint?"
She says yes, or no, is an actress, "Can't you tell by how well I
do the modeling part? and can't work right now and have to pay
the bills and got bored sick with those temp jobs," and I say "But
this doesn't pay as well, does it?" "Pays enough and gives me
plenty of time to think and memorize scripts—what do you do?"
and just as I'm about to say, art instructor calls out "Five minutes
are up, model," she poses, alternates looking at the clock and me
as she does, returns to talk during the next break, bathrobe now
fastened at the top, so I can't as I want see in, which she might

have caught me doing last time, I tell her what I do, she compliments me for not just having lunch on my lunch hour— "I admire people, no matter how old, who are always extending themselves, trying out new things and not getting stale, you know?" I say "Thanks, and you might think this presumptuous—after all, we've only spoken for two short breaks," and I pause, say "No, it's silly, besides wrong," and she says "What is?—go on, I might be so sweaty and smelly next break you might not want to continue this conversation, which I find a nice relief from the silent stony posing," and I ask if she'd like to have coffee after class, she says she has another class right after, "so another time maybe?" "When?" I say, she tells me when she'll be free, I say I'll still be working then, she says "Then when do you get off and I can probably meet you in front of your office building if it's not too late, for something as long as dinner I'm not really interested in," I say, we meet, coffee, she has tea, go out, stay in, out, in, make love, her name's Jane, when she told me I said "That's remarkable," she asked why and I said "Oh, it's just that I guessed it the moment I saw you there on the modeling platform," I call her J for short, move in, marry, children, bed, watch, getting them up, years, city, country, sickness, death, exercise, shower, shave, newspaper, no news, old news, turn to the reviews, my kids whom I kiss good-night every night, when they're awake and later when they're sleeping.

SUSAN BURMEISTER
Pressing Tight

He spent the first few minutes straightening the tines of his fork, pressing his point, pressing the tines. Charlotte felt the pressing and steadied her hand on the edge of the square table. Finally he set his fork aside and stared at her full in the face. She pulled her lavender sweater tightly around her and held it closed with her left hand, sipping Earl Grey with her right, refusing his eyes.

"I can't accept that it's over, Charlotte," Ray said for the third time since they'd sat down. The waitress had seated them at a good table, the only one by a window that did not get cold gusts every time the front door opened. "I understand you need more time to yourself, I can understand that. We've been spending nearly every hour together since we met in June. But why not take the time, an extra hour or so in the evenings, and leave us be? Why does it have to be flat-out over?" He gave his fork a hard twist, bending its narrow neck over to one side. "Can't accept that, Charlotte." He looked up at her, catching her eyes by surprise and holding onto them. "I'm sorry."

This was looking to be a scene, and Charlotte uncrossed her

legs and set both feet on the nice linoleum. Ray was a man of strong opinions, but she'd never seen him this edgy in their five months of going together. She hadn't counted on this kind of reaction from him. All she'd brought up was about needing more time to herself, about wanting to take things a little slower, and she had thought he'd adjust to that over a few weeks and then finally she'd ease on out altogether. It wasn't that odd of a thing to do. Certainly she'd done it before with other men, more than once. This kind of fork-bending and twisty faces, as though he were being bodily hurt, she hadn't counted on anything like that. It seemed best not to speak.

"You notice I'm not smoking as much as I used to, since you told me it made your eyes sting. I pretty much stopped, really. Almost right away." He paused while their waitress filled his coffee cup again. "You noticed that? How I took care of that right away once I knew?"

Seeing Charlotte nod, he went on, "You see, all you have to do with me is tell me what the problems are, tell me where I'm going wrong, and I'll fix it. Right away. If it's my calls to you in the mornings that are hemming you in, just say so. I can cut back to every other day, or talk shorter, or whatever it is you need. You just give the word."

Charlotte's hands were cold, and the face on her watch had slipped onto the far side of her wrist. Her wrists always shrunk up when she was cold. She couldn't see what time it was without twisting her watch back around. She let it be. Folks were lining up for supper already and it had gotten completely black outside, so it had to be close to six o'clock. They'd been there ever since she'd gotten off work.

"I want you to make me a list, Charlotte. A full list of everything you need me to fix about myself. Do it up tonight. I swear I'll check off each thing before you know it. By Christmas. Sooner even. Give me a week and I'll fix it all. Do the list up tonight. I'll come by your work tomorrow on my lunch break, you can give me the list, maybe we can get a pizza or something, and I'll read it over right then, right while they're making the pizza. That way I can ask you about any of the things I don't understand, or ask you for examples. Like if you write down that I'm too messy, maybe I'd want to ask if you meant about my car, which I'm already working on, by the way. I've moved all the stuff in there into the trunk, so the regular inside part is much better. You'll see tonight when I drive you home."

He put another pack of sugar into his half-drunk cup and stirred it in with the handle of his fork, tines standing erect on its broken neck.

"You make me up that list and I swear to you, Charlotte, I swear to you, I'll fix every single thing. I'll make it right."

She could feel him scraping the back of her eyes with his own, looking for something, raking the tender tissue over and over again.

"I wish you would look at me the way you used to early on. It's been a long time since I've seen that look in your eye, that look that pulled me into you. That look that said, 'Come inside, Ray, you're safe here. Come be with me.' See, that's a good way of putting it. I went for you, all-out went for you, told everyone about you from day one, made you my life—lock, stock, and barrel. And I threw away the key. You try to tell me you want me out of your life, but you see, I'm in your life. No, that's not even it. I'm in you. You're me. I'm you. It's like it's me wearing that purple sweater right now."

Charlotte caught sight of the wall clock reflected in the window. It took her a moment to flip it around backward in her head, so she could tell what time it was. Six-twenty. If she left now, right now, she would make the six-thirty-five bus. She was still looking at the clock face in the window when she saw something moving outside.

It was not outside. It was Ray's bulk shaking, and she heard his moist, broken sounds.

She watched his reflected shape as he laid his head down on his arms, still clutching the handle of the twisted fork in his left hand, its tines now pointing directly at her.

She got up without knocking the table, grabbed her coat and purse from the back of her chair, and hurried out the door and around the corner. As she came to the window by Ray, she slowed. She saw him look up, saw him roam the room with his eyes, tears stopped in panic. Finally he turned and spotted her on the other side of the glass.

He quickly pressed his right hand flat against the window, and Charlotte hesitated. This was a ritual they had, pressing their hands together like that when they were saying good-bye. Charlotte put her left hand up to the window and matched it to his. Suddenly Ray removed his hand and got halfway up out of his chair, craning his head to reach the window. He began tracing her fingers through the glass with his tongue, licking finger-sized strips of window clean. He closed his eyes then, his tongue pasted to the center of her palm.

Charlotte lifted her hand from the window, leaving her fingers splayed in the brisk air, and stared for a moment at the pink pad of wet flesh pressed tight to the pane, squeezed white at its tip, ringed with steam.

Cradling her left hand in her right, she ran all the way to the six-thirty-five.

B MULLIGAN
1991

Well, look what's coming!

Women cry, even in their worst pain, with hope and relief. They cry like wolves and coyotes do, howling to talk to their mates as well as to the rest of the pack. But there is something about the way men cry that sounds so hopeless, so anguished, as though the very act of crying is killing them.

...I wrap my arms tighter around Ernie, touching with my fingertips the scars and pointed shrapnel still under his skin. He nuzzles his face deep into the crook of my neck to hide it while he cries.

from "Angel" by Mary Ellis

Naturally, Cherry and Rose became best friends. From the very first day, they did everything together. They jumped rope, played jacks, and played hopscotch together. They were good at things by themselves, but together, they were even better.

from "The Flower Girls" by Lawson Fusao Inada

"Come here, Gracie. I want to show you something." Just take her down there and turn on the light. She knew what Gracie would say.

"Holy shit, Leola! He didn't!"

from "Prized Possessions" by Robert Abel

A green leaf has absorbed all color rays except green. The rays we name green are reflected back. We specify an object by the one quality it has rejected and hurled in our faces.

from "Chips and Whetstones" by Susan J. Alenick

160